Monster Lovin'

Smutty, Spine-Tingling Queer Stories

S. PARK

Microcosm Publishing
Portland, Ore | Cleveland, OH

MONSTER LOVIN'
Smutty, Spine-Tingling Queer Stories

© 2023 S. Park
© This edition Microcosm Publishing 2023
First edition - 2,000 copies - August 22, 2023
ISBN 9781648411519
This is Microcosm #791
Cover by Gerta O. Egy

To join the ranks of high-class stores that feature Microcosm titles, talk to your local rep: In the U.S. **COMO** (Atlantic), **ABRAHAM** (Midwest), **BOB BARNETT** (Texas, Oklahoma, Louisiana, Arkansas), **IMPRINT** (Pacific), **TURNAROUND** (Europe), **UTP/MANDA** (Canada), **NEW SOUTH** (Australia/New Zealand), **GPS** in Asia, Africa, India, South America, and other countries, or **FAIRE** in the gift trade.

For a catalog, write or visit:
Microcosm Publishing
2752 N Williams Ave.
Portland, OR 97227
https://microcosm.pub/QueeringConsent

Did you know that you can buy our books directly from us at sliding scale rates? Support a small, independent publisher and pay less than Amazon's price at **www.Microcosm.Pub**

Library of Congress Publication Data
Names: Park, S., 1978- author.
Title: Monster lovin' : smutty, spine-tingling queer stories / by S. Park (author).

Description: [Portland, OR] : Microcosm Publishing, [2023] | Series: Queering consent | Summary: "Have you ever considered the erotic possibilities of loving an ancient being of incredibly inhuman power? The monstrous becomes familiar and profoundly pleasurable in S. Park's new collection of m/m queer, consensual erotica. Tentacles find their way into every crevice, a sexy stranger turns out to be part plant, part man, and a powerful demon cuddles up in bed. In these tender, sweaty, high-heat stories, horror turns to delight, the monster always turns out to be worthy of love . . . and sometimes, the monster turns out to be you"-- Provided by publisher.
Identifiers: LCCN 2023007023 | ISBN 9781648411519 (trade paperback)
Subjects: LCGFT: Erotic fiction. | Monster fiction. | Queer fiction. | Gay fiction. | Short stories.
Classification: LCC PS3616.A74359 M66 2023 | DDC 813/.6--dc23/eng/20230313
LC record available at https://lccn.loc.gov/2023007023

MICROCOSM · PUBLISHING

MICROCOSM PUBLISHING is Portland's most diversified publishing house and distributor, with a focus on the colorful, authentic, and empowering. Our books and zines have put your power in your hands since 1996, equipping readers to make positive changes in their lives and in the world around them. Microcosm emphasizes skill-building, showing hidden histories, and fostering creativity through challenging conventional publishing wisdom with books and bookettes about DIY skills, food, bicycling, gender, self-care, and social justice. What was once a distro and record label started by Joe Biel in a drafty bedroom was determined to be *Publishers Weekly's* fastest-growing publisher of 2022 and #3 in 2023, and is now among the oldest independent publishing houses in Portland, OR, and Cleveland, OH. We are a politically moderate, centrist publisher in a world that has inched to the right for the past 80 years.

Global labor conditions are bad, and our roots in industrial Cleveland in the '70s and '80s made us appreciate the need to treat workers right. Therefore, our books are **MADE IN THE USA**.

CONTENTS

Introduction

There's something inherently queer about mixing the human and the inhuman. In everything from the famous Japanese print *The Dream of the Fisherman's Wife*, depicting a woman being pleasured by an octopus, to *The Shape of Water*, with its modern spin on much the same theme, seeing humans love monsters feels queer even when the pairing is theoretically straight.

LGBTQ+ people have often been viewed by the mainstream as shocking, strange, and even monstrous, so perhaps that's not surprising. Also unsurprising is how various creators have used queerness in appearance or behavior to make their villains stranger, more monstrous, more other.

Likewise far from shocking is the way queer people—whose various labels, from "gay" to "dyke" to "queer" itself, were all originally slurs and insults—often embrace the monstrous. If we can't be seen as wholesome and normal, well then, let us have fun being as strange and wild and even villainous as we can be.

Of course that's all subtext, not text. Is *The Lion King*'s Scar meant to be gay? Was Lovecraft including LGBTQ+ people in his horrors beyond human comprehension? One can see the possible intent, but I've always preferred clear text over subtext. So when a Lovecraftian monstrosity is revealed in the coming pages, you will not have to wonder if the being from beyond the stars is gay; you will already have met his boyfriend before the first tentacle appears.

Someday we may live in a world where queer people are fully accepted and not seen as the other, and I think that will be wonderful. But here and now, in the world we have, I will take every scrap of joy I can from embracing my queer, monstrous self, tentacles and all.

Incubus

"**I**'m not sure you really understand what you're asking for, angel," said Bezial, trying not to fidget where he sat on a tatty old couch in Anton's study. He'd first met Anton in said study, when the then-young scholar had summoned him. Anton had meant to summon an imp, merely to test the spell he'd found in one of the countless books he collected, which lined every bit of the study's walls, the shelves even covering what had once been windows. He'd gotten the much more powerful Bezial instead.

Not that Bezial currently looked like an ancient being of impossibly inhuman power. He currently looked like a perfectly ordinary man, middling in height and build and coloration, utterly unremarkable save for the bright red eyes with their slit pupils that his shape-shifting couldn't hide. All demons had one little tell, somewhere, no matter what form they took, and those were his.

Anton sat opposite him on an equally decrepit armchair, a glass of wine in his hand. Its twin was on a coffee table between the pair, and was empty. Bezial could hold his booze much better than his human companion, though Anton was the one who loved things like wine, like food, like all the various bodily pleasures a man might enjoy.

Time had changed the scrawny young scholar who'd summoned Bezial into a comfortably padded man of middle age: fair, fly-away hair in an untidy halo, the pale color hiding the generous streaks of gray.

"I am not as young as I used to be, my dear." Anton smiled at Bezial over the top of his wine glass, his expression cheerfully conspiratorial. "I rather know what making love is by now. I've done it a few times, even, when the occasion seemed appropriate."

Bezial scowled and tried not to feel jealous of Anton's past partners. He had a point to make here. "Demons don't 'make love,' Anton. Demons *fuck*."

"I rather think those are both euphemisms for the same thing. Sex is sex, dear, and I think we're at a point where it's rather on the table. Though I'd prefer my bedroom, but if you're so inclined . . ." He rapped his knuckles on the table beside his chair with a twinkle in his eye.

Bezial shook his head. He could feel his cheeks flushing, but he had to let Anton know what he was in for if they took this next step. Kissing and holding hands was all well and good, but this . . . "Sex isn't always just sex, necessarily. When I . . . feel something for my partner it's hard to keep in control of myself. Of my . . . nature." He dared to look into Anton's eyes as he said, "Given how strongly I feel about you, I'm afraid I'd lose control completely. I don't want to hurt you."

"Oh, Bezial." Anton's smile was practically radiant, his plump cheeks flushed a lovely pink. "That's incredibly sweet. Surely there's no need to worry, though."

"You're the person I love," said Bezial, feeling odd saying those words. Demons weren't even supposed to *like* mortal humans. "I'd die if I ever hurt you."

"But you won't. Die or hurt me." Anton smiled serenely. "I trust you completely. You've been in a position to yank my guts out countless times now, and you've never harmed me. And anyway, ah . . ." Anton blushed charmingly, in a way that made Bezial perk up and pay attention.

"Hmm?"

"I am actually quite certain that if you did hurt me just a little, I would like it."

Bezial suddenly found himself blushing even more brightly than Anton. ". . . what?"

Anton actually giggled. "Some people do like pain as part of sex, you know. Or have you never heard of sadomasochism?"

"I've heard of it," Bezial said shortly, feeling suddenly quite out of his depth. He'd had plenty of sex, but his ideas of mixing things up had more to do with taking advantage of being able to change his body up a bit. He'd never played with any of *that* sort of thing.

"There's some de Sade up there," said Anton, gesturing at a particular bookshelf. "He's a bit of a nut, really. But if you take the things he wrote as pure fantasy, some of them are quite . . . interesting."

". . . fuck," said Bezial, feeling entirely off balance.

Anton giggled again. "We can use a safeword. Red, yellow, green, you know those?"

Bezial, still mentally reeling, managed a nod.

"That way I can let you know if you're hurting me in a bad way. But really, my love, I've wanted to make love to you—or to fuck, whichever way you'd rather—for ages now. If you're interested in me that way, I'm most definitely not going to let a little demonic nature creeping in rob me of the chance to share that with you. I know what you are. I've always known, and it doesn't bother me one whit." He smiled and cupped Bezial's cheek in his hand, running his thumb along the cheekbone, just under Bezial's crimson dragon's eye. Bezial melted into the touch, into Anton's trust and acceptance. He'd always hated how he couldn't hide his eyes, but somewhere along the line he'd stopped minding Anton seeing them. Perhaps it could be that way with the rest of him, too.

"Alright," said Bezial, feeling a shiver of mingled fear and desire go through him. "If . . . if you're sure."

"Very sure, love," said Anton, gently but firmly.

"Right." Bezial started undoing buttons. Anton only sat back in his chair and watched as Bezial stripped. The demon wasn't trying to hurry, but it wasn't a strip tease either. He was simply undressing, and there was an occasional tremor that made him fumble a button. His stomach felt like a solid knot of nervousness. He was about to be seen naked.

There was naked, and then there was *naked*, and he couldn't even remember the last time he'd let anybody see him showing any demonic features that he could possibly hide. Now he was about to show Anton quite a lot more than just his eyes, and no matter how much he trusted his keeper, friend, and, lately, love, it was still nerve-wracking to do.

He finally got everything shed and set aside, and he let some of his human nature slip away. He didn't go all the way, not yet. He eased into being physically demonic, just a little.

His wings were the most obvious thing, black shadows unfolding behind him, but Anton had at least seen those before. Bezial's demon nature was partly draconic, so the scales scattered in odd little patches here and there were the next most visible change. His nails were halfway to claws too, though, and he had very small horns, almost invisible in the dark tangle of his hair. His eyes were crimson from one side to the other, no white showing at all, the pupils broad black pits in the dim light of the study, and when he gave Anton an almost shy smile, then licked his lips nervously, it showed a pair of fangs and a nearly human tongue with a fork at the tip.

"This is . . . some of it," he said, hesitantly.

"May I?" said Anton, rising.

"Uhm. Yes?" Bezial didn't know what he'd just agreed to, but he was willing to give Anton whatever he wanted.

The human scholar reached out and traced a finger down Bezial's arm, over a patch of dark scales there. Bezial shivered. The scales were less sensitive than skin, but the touch sent tingles through him all the same.

"Fascinating," said Anton softly. "The dragon thing isn't just a form you take, then?"

Bezial shrugged. "It's kinda integral. Lotta demons have an animal association."

Anton nodded, still stroking that little patch of scales. "And here I am, a boring human, with no other nature than my own."

"I don't mind," said Bezial.

Anton smiled. "I'm glad you don't. Still, this is much more interesting." He took Bezial's hand, rubbing a thumb curiously over one sharp talon. "Much more interesting," he murmured again, and the pink on his cheeks spread further. Bezial licked his lips, feeling something hot stir in him, something that was both very human and entirely inhuman at once. He stared into Anton's wide hazel eyes, and thought that this night was about to get very, very interesting indeed.

———•———•———•———

Anton felt nearly mesmerized by Bezial, just as something small and fluffy might be mesmerized by a serpent. It was far from an unpleasant feeling, making his heart beat just that much faster, mixing an excitement that was like fear, but wasn't, with an excitement that was definitely arousal.

Bezial lifted the hand that Anton wasn't holding and drew one pointed nail down the human's cheek. Anton went utterly still save for a faint tremor, his heart suddenly beating even faster at the touch of that razor-sharp claw. Bezial chuckled and continued, drawing it down his neck to his collar. "You're still dressed," said Bezial softly, and Anton twitched.

"Ah, yes, indeed. Shall I, ah, do something about that?"

"Unless you want me to claw it off of you, yes." Bezial's voice had gone darker, deeper, and it sent an utterly thrilling shudder through Anton. He was intensely aware now that Bezial was a *demon*, was nothing like human, and that awareness was setting him on fire. He could feel the ache between his legs, and his undershorts were already growing damp. It normally took him quite some time to get into such a state, but it had happened in no time at all tonight.

Anton started undoing his bowtie with rather unseemly haste, suddenly needing very much to be as naked as the demon was. Bezial leaned against a bookshelf, lounging there, and watched as Anton stripped as swiftly as a man wearing so many layers and with so many buttons could.

Once he got down to his undershorts, though, Anton paused. What Bezial had just said, about having them clawed off, ran through his mind. He felt himself flushing hotly, one hand on the drawstring that held them, but then he let his hand fall, merely standing there, the damp patch between his legs very much evident.

Bezial stepped towards him, and Anton had the thought that they must make a strange couple just now. The tall—perhaps even taller than he'd been a moment ago?—muscular, lean Bezial, wings out, dusted with scales, very obviously nothing like human, and Anton, entirely human, and a plump, pink little human at that. Then Bezial's wings were folding around him, and his arms as well, his lips finding Anton's. The kiss was rough and forceful, the demon pressing his forked tongue into Anton's mouth, twisting it around his own aggressively, possessively. They'd kissed before, but never like this. Anton shuddered in Bezial's embrace, pressing to him, feeling skin and scales, wrapped in the black shadows of his wings. He'd meant to suggest they go up to his bedroom but he was nearly ready to beg Bezial to take him right here on the study floor, and any damage to the books be damned!

Nearly, but not quite. He couldn't quite brace himself to actually consider harm to his precious collection. So, when Bezial finally let him up for air, Anton gasped, "Upstairs?"

Bezial, eyes very wide, stared at him as if having trouble understanding the word for a moment, then nodded. "Right. Yes." His voice was still deep and rough, and Anton shivered again and nearly scurried up to the flat above the study. Bezial was right on his heels, and there was a sense of being *pursued* that made Anton shiver even more.

This was utterly *amazing*.

Anton had cleaned and made up his bed earlier that day, in hopeful anticipation. Now he was very glad he had, for there was nothing to do but step into the room. He didn't even make it all the way to the bed, quite, before he was caught from behind, Bezial's long arms wrapping around him, and he found the demon nipping at his shoulder with sharp fangs.

"Oh my!" He could feel Bezial as a firm, angular hardness against his back, and one hardness in particular was grinding against his backside. Bezial's hands held him tight, claws biting into his upper arms, and he nipped up the side of Anton's neck, not hard enough to break the skin, but it would probably leave marks. Anton moaned helplessly, completely caught up in it.

A moment later Bezial let go, but only to shove Anton forward, onto the bed. Anton didn't resist that at all; he only crawled a little further up onto the bed and turned around, to see Bezial crawling after him, his eyes fixed on Anton, pupils so broad they were pits of black with only a thin ring of red around the edges of them.

"Oh." Anton found he was panting, drawing in short, shuddering gasps of air. His body was full of electric heat, nearly terror, not terror *at all*, as Bezial, fangs bared, forked tongue licking his lips, crawled atop him. Bezial's claws caught at Anton's shorts and tugged, tore, shredded them completely, though the sharp claws barely even touched Anton's skin. Bezial tossed the ruined fabric aside, letting the room's cool air wash over Anton's private parts, over the curled hair there, damp with arousal, the parted lips of his cunt, and the little nub of a cock that peeked from between them. The demon dove on it immediately, and Anton cried out in shock once, then again, and then a third time at an overwhelming series of sensations: a hot swipe of a tongue over him, a terrifying and glorious nip of fangs against his lips and then, oh dear *lord*, that tongue burrowing inside him.

He found his hands fisting in the demon's hair without even having meant to, and his body was arching and shuddering as the pleasure of it raced through him.

Bezial lifted his head from Anton's cunt and the human let out a soft whimper of disappointment as the wonderful sensation went away. The demon licked his lips with a long, forked tongue that was now nothing like human. "Anton, pleasssssssssssssse," he hissed, crawling further up over Anton, "Want . . . *need* you . . ." His voice was thick, as if he were having trouble even knowing how to speak, even being capable of speech. His body was slipping further from human, scales spreading, horns now a sweeping arch back over hair that had become long and tangled.

"Oh yes," said Anton, breathlessly, and then Bezial was on him again, pushing his tongue into Anton's mouth, nipping at Anton's lips, and down the side of his neck, covering him with a flurry of rough kisses and dangerously sharp love bites. His body pressed down on Anton, a firm weight, a cool pressure, serpentine, strange, wonderful. Anton slid his hands down Bezial's back, feeling the sleek scales under his fingers, touching where the wings joined his body and the leathery membrane was soft and warm, feeling all the textures of him, taking in the inhumanness of him and reveling in it.

Bezial growled, low in the back of his throat, and ground his hips down on Anton. He was breathing fast and harsh, his wings fanning the air slowly behind him. The angel could feel the demon's cock grinding against him and knew that Bezial's member must have changed too, for it felt strange, and not just for the coolness of it. Then he realized that he was feeling something else, a second hardness pushing between his legs, and a shudder went through him. He knew enough about scaled things to know what that must be. "Oh my."

Bezial only growled again in response, grinding harder against Anton, one cock grinding against Anton's cunt, the other angled lower, thrusting between Anton's thighs. Still growling and nipping at Anton's shoulder, Bezial began thrusting as if he meant to continue like this, just find his pleasure in simple, mindless friction, but Anton wanted more.

"Yellow, my lovely demon. My dear, sweet creature. Hold a moment, please."

Bezial huffed in the back of his throat, but pulled back, still looming over Anton on hands and knees, but allowing enough space, enough time, enough breath between them for Anton to do the thing that had immediately sprung into his mind on discovering there were two marvelous reptilian cocks present. He glanced down at them, seeing the flesh flushed so dark it was almost purple on both of them, shaped entirely unlike human cocks, swelling at their bases, blunt on their heads, ridged interestingly along the upper side of each, and each glistening from tip to root with slick.

Glad—in a way he'd never quite been before—of how his body was made, Anton shifted under Bezial, drawing his knees up, offering himself. "Let's find a home for both those lovely, lovely things, shall we, my wonderful demon?"

"Anton," growled Bezial, and though it was still a low, inhuman sound, it was sweet and needy and utterly perfect. Anton grabbed the upper of the marvelous pair of cocks and guided it as Bezial lowered himself, pressing the head of it to his cunt, which was so very wet and ready for it.

Bezial's head pushed in easily, perfectly, and he moved as if to sink in further, but Anton murmured, "Hold still, love," and Bezial froze, save for his rapid panting. Anton wrapped his hand around the second cock, wringing a choked moan from Bezial, and guided the head of that below, positioning the hard, slick tip of it at his backside and making an effort to relax.

Bezial gasped at the feel of it against him and bucked his hips forward, obviously unable to help himself. "Yessss . . ."

"Yes love, yes, just like that. You feel so wonderful in me." Bezial did. Anton had used a toy or two in his life, and the sensation of being doubly filled with one had been nice when he'd tried it, but this was miles beyond "nice." The demon sank into him swiftly, not thrusting in, not quite, but burying himself eagerly, the cock in Anton's cunt filling him perfectly, the one in his ass stretching him to the point of pain in the best way. His breath was hot against Anton's ear, and he bit there, sharp fangs almost delicate, just the barest sting of them pricking. Anton ran his hands down Bezial's back again, just under the wings, over his hips, down to his ass, and Bezial ground down harder, pushing his cocks as deep as possible, stretching Anton out with the swollen bases of them.

"Yes," said Anton as he was filled more utterly than he'd ever been. "Yes, oh yes."

"Yessssss," echoed Bezial. "Yesss, my love. Mine, ssssss . . ." Bezial shuddered where he rested within Anton, but did not move.

Anton's fingers dug into the spare flesh of Bezial, trying to encourage him. "I'm yours, my demon, my love, my beautiful creature. I'm yours, and I want you to take me. Please, don't hold back."

There was another huff, disbelieving, and Bezial buried his face in the sweet spot between Anton's neck and shoulder, his whole body trembling.

"Please, Bezial," said Anton. There was just a tiny pause, and then Bezial pulled back and thrust in, pushing both cocks into the human beneath him deep and hard. Anton gasped, pleasure that was twined with pain shocking through him.

Bezial growled again, a deep rumble, and repeated the thrust, if anything even harder this time. Then again, and again, settling swiftly into a steady, primal rhythm, bottoming out on both sides each time, making Anton moan and writhe beneath him. It was so good, so wonderfully good, so intense and strange and so very *Bezial*, something no human being could ever have given him.

It was too wonderful to hold back, in fact. Anton's body tensed, pleasure building. He knew he was on the edge of coming, and he gripped Bezial's shoulders, his fingers digging in. "Oh Bezial. Oh yes . . . More, my love. Yes, oh yes!"

Bezial pressed a hot kiss on him, his long, forked tongue slithering into Anton's mouth, filling it as the rest of him was filled, pushing deep, denying him breath. His body trembled with it, desperate for air, but even more desperate for the thing that rose in him, building and building until it crashed over him and with a silent, helpless shudder he came intensely, the world going white around him.

He clenched as hard as he could on Bezial as his orgasm washed through him, able to hold on to just enough conscious thought to know he wanted Bezial there with him, wanted his wonderful demonic lover to feel this same thing, and so he tightened himself and lifted his hips, clinging to Bezial as he tried to bring his beloved to his peak as well.

Bezial pulled back from the kiss, panting hard, claws digging into Anton's back. The human gasped in a desperate breath as the demon buried his face against Anton's shoulder, his thrusts becoming rough, jerky, barely pulling out but still slamming in deep enough to hurt in the best possible way, and then with a wordless cry he too was there, flooding Anton with a double load of hot seed, his black wings stretching so wide that one of them managed to hit the only bookshelf in the room, sending books tumbling. But for once Anton cared nothing whatsoever for his precious volumes, all he knew was the primal heat of it as Bezial filled him at last.

After a small eternity they both lay together, Bezial still doubly buried inside Anton, nuzzling at his shoulder where he'd left marks that would definitely turn to bruises later, Anton drawing his hands lightly up and down Bezial's sides, over the scales there, eyes half closed in dreamy contentment.

It was some time before Bezial said, his voice still a little rough, a little sibilant, "Wasss that . . . okay?"

"Bezial, my dearest demon, I am something of a connoisseur of various pleasures of the flesh, and that was quite possibly the most wonderful thing I've felt in my entire life." He shifted one hand to stroke along Bezial's hair, combing his fingers gently through the dark tangle of it. "It was much more than merely okay."

Bezial sighed in something like relief. "I'm . . . glad." He let his own eyes slide closed, his head resting on Anton's shoulder. After a while he shifted, drawing his wings in, and said, hesitantly, "I can . . . change back, if you want."

"Only if you'll be more comfortable," said Anton. "I'm quite fine like this. This is lovely." Bezial's cocks were softer than they'd been, but they still filled him wonderfully, and Anton felt that he'd be perfectly content to lie here until the sun burned out and the world came to an end. The human scholar continued to stroke Bezial's hair slowly, and Bezial made a sound that was half hiss and half purr, a stuttering "sssrrrrrsssrrr" of utter relaxation.

"I love you, my sweet, demonic creature," murmured Anton softly.

"I love you too," was Bezial's drowsy reply, and they then were asleep, human and demon, still joined together.

Gut Feeling

*A*egeus carefully set the silvery tray on a side table by the fireplace, and surveyed everything, checking for at least the fourth time that he hadn't forgotten anything. The checking was foolish; he'd made a list of necessary items on his phone months ago, when the urge had started to become maddening, and now that it had gone beyond maddening to something that might be called all-consuming, Aegeus had followed the list to the letter.

The crackling fire shed a warm glow over the room, casting the further corners in shadow, but clearly illuminating the sheepskin rug where Aegeus knelt. He knew that what he was about to do was more usually done in white, sterile rooms filled with bright lights, but then it was also usually done by doctors, for medical reasons, not by madmen for reasons of bizarre compulsive obsession.

No. He wasn't mad. He *had* to do this. It would work. It must work. He couldn't bear it if it didn't work.

Aegeus shook his head and stripped his shirt off, baring a pale-skinned, chubby, nearly hairless torso. He put a hand over his belly, pressing into the soft give of it, and bit his lip. He swore he could feel something squirm eagerly under his hand.

Maybe it was just a delusion. How could there be anything beneath his skin but the same ordinary organs he'd seen countless times in illustrations and little plastic models?

Yet if it was a delusion, it was one he'd given himself over to completely.

He ran his eyes over the tray a final time, taking in the sterilizing wipes, the roll of paper towels, the self-sticking medical tape, the stack of gauze pads, and finally the scalpel, gleaming like gold in the firelight.

His fingers touched the cold handle, and his whole body gave a shudder. It should have been a shudder of fear, but it wasn't; it was a shudder of eagerness.

Time to begin.

●——————●——————●

"Christopher Aegeus McCausland! You haven't cleaned your plate!"

Aegeus, who had never in his life gone by Christopher or even Chris when given the choice, gave his mother an incredulous look. "I'm sixteen Mom, not six. And you know I have digestive issues. What the heck?"

"I made this specifically for you. Isn't lasagna your favorite?"

"Zucchini lasagna is, Mom." Aegeus poked at his plate with his fork. He'd picked around the ground beef as much as he could, but other than picking out all the big noodle sheets, there had been only so much he could do.

"This vegetarian phase of yours . . ." His mother—adoptive, and he'd have put that aside if he could, but she didn't let him—glared at him sternly over her own plate.

"Mom! It's not a phase, and I'm not vegetarian, but red meat upsets my stomach. You know that."

"After I cooked it just for you, you're leaving half of it there?" she said, avoiding his explanation entirely. "I do so much for you! Your father and I didn't have to adopt you, you know. Everyone wants babies, but you were five, and you probably wouldn't have a home if we hadn't taken you in."

"Mom . . ." Aegeus didn't know what to say. He hated her bringing that up. He had no memories from before he'd been adopted, only the memory of his name. Which they'd changed, though they'd at least kept the old name as a middle name. But he only heard it from his parents when he was in trouble. Without any memory of his former life, though, he could have felt like just another kid, in another normal family, if his parents would just *let* him.

"Just eat it, son, or you'll be grounded," broke in his father, who was polishing off his own plate. Aegeus's three younger siblings, all also adopted, kept their heads down and said nothing, meekly forking up their own lasagna.

Mom could sometimes be argued around, but if Dad said it, it was happening. Aegeus weighed an unpleasant visit to the bathroom against days without his computer or game consoles, and with a sigh took up a forkful of beef.

It tasted okay. Not great, but the flavor itself didn't make him feel sick.

As soon as that first bite hit his stomach, though, the protest started. Sometimes he thought he should visit a doctor about it, but the one time he'd brought up the subject his dad had actually *shouted*. His parents both seemed to think that his digestive problems were something he did on purpose. As if he *wanted* to vomit all the time! He'd have loved being able to eat a burger or a pepperoni pizza or any number of other things without trouble.

With his mother watching, Aegeus managed to swallow most of what he'd left on his plate. A few bites remained when he put down his fork and said, "May I be excused?"

"You may."

Aegeus rose, then nearly bolted to the bathroom, his entire abdomen feeling like a churning, bubbling mess. Reaching the toilet, Aegeus bent over and vomited with the efficiency of long experience. He then rinsed his mouth and spat before making his way upstairs to his bedroom. As he walked he no longer felt sick, but he did still feel like his insides were clenching and churning, wiggling around uncomfortably within.

He thought, sometimes, that there was something in there, something that had grown slowly over the years, since as a little kid he'd been able to eat nearly anything. Now it seemed he added a new food to the "no go" list every few months.

What would happen if eventually he couldn't eat anything? What would he do?

No, it would never get to that point. If nothing else, there was always fruit. He loved fruit. He'd never had even the least twinge from any fruit. Heck, the tomato was a big part of why he liked lasagna, though the cheese and the rest certainly played a part. But he could eat any kind of fruit all day long and never feel the least bit sick. If it were up to him, he'd live on it and nothing else.

But it wasn't up to him. At least not yet. Soon, though. His grades were very good, and in two more years he'd be at college, hopefully living on his own in an apartment or at least in the dorms. Then he could eat whatever he wanted. Then maybe he could stop feeling so sick all the time.

———————•———————•———————•———————

Aegeus picked up the scalpel, staring at the impossibly thin edge of it in a kind of horrified fascination. It was finer than a razor, by quite a bit. There was no question that it would cut easily into him.

Could he actually do this?

Should he actually do this?

What else was he supposed to do, though? He no longer vomited all the time, not since he'd gotten out on his own years ago and had been able to eat what he liked. And yet the churning, squirming, weird discomfort was now nearly constant. And then there was his bizarre weight gain—he shouldn't have become this size living on nothing but fruit—and the constantly increasing certainly that there was *something* inside him that wanted out. It was making his life into what felt like a nightmare, even though on the surface he was doing well.

His parents had stopped supporting him when he'd come out as bisexual in his third year of college, but he'd gotten himself through, and was making a good living in network administration now. He wasn't rich, by any means, but he had a nice little condo, a brand new company car, and all the strawberries he could eat.

Yet that all seemed to vanish in the face of his certainty that something wasn't right, that something was trapped, growing inside him. He'd started to worry that if he didn't let it out it would burst from him, like the creature in *Alien*, and somehow damage both him and the whatever-it-was in the process.

A scalpel cut would surely be better than a ragged tear, right?

And maybe once the thing inside him was out he'd feel better about everything else that worried him too. Oh, maybe not his occasional work conflicts or the worries that had to do with the state of the world, but it felt like his personal life, his private life, would be so good, so right, once there was no longer something tightly squirming within him.

He placed the scalpel where he knew he needed to begin, the point hovering mere millimeters above the skin below his sternum, where it could cut open his soft belly and lay bare whatever might be inside.

Surely everything would be better after he'd done it. Surely.

⋅•⋅•⋅•⋅

It was strange. That was all Aegeus could think as Jayden moved above him. The other young man was panting, letting out occasional low groans as he thrust, obviously very much enjoying himself.

Aegeus had expected to enjoy himself. Or to hate it. But instead all he could do was feel a detached, clinical sort of indifference. Being filled with a hard, thick cock felt unusual, that was all. It was a different sensation, neither good nor bad.

That was frustrating. He *liked* Jayden. They'd been roommates his first year of college, friends his second, and Jayden had offered to be fuckbuddies not long after Aegeus had come out.

Trying out gay sex with somebody he liked and trusted—and who was on the university gymnastics team too, so had an amazing body, tons of flexibility, and all kinds of stamina—had seemed like a great idea.

Aegeus had even gotten turned on in the earlier parts of things, with the kissing and the touching. This, though, was somehow almost boring. It wasn't even keeping his mind off his weird stomach issues; he could feel the wiggling as much as he usually did.

Ugh.

Of course he had to be made all wrong for this too.

Well, at least he was bottoming. Imagine if he'd gotten this bored trying to top! But he wasn't very well endowed, and he'd been more than willing to try out getting penetrated. The idea had seemed like a good one. Yet something about the execution wasn't right, somehow. He didn't know what was wrong with it, exactly. It wasn't as though anything hurt, or that he disliked anything. In fact he was still very much enjoying the little sounds Jayden was making above him.

With a sigh Aegeus clenched down on Jayden's cock. It still didn't do anything for him, but Jayden groaned and started thrusting faster, which was nice.

Maybe he was asexual? He'd never been able to come with a woman either, after all. That was part of why he'd started exploring his feelings about men. It had seemed like something was missing when he was with a woman. But whatever it was, it was missing now too. So perhaps he simply wasn't meant for sex.

But he'd found Jayden attractive. He'd gotten turned on earlier. It was the sex itself that was wrong.

Eventually Jayden came, but then he insisted on trying to make Aegeus come, and Aegeus knew that would be futile and go nowhere. Hell, he could barely get off masturbating; that had never been satisfying at all. He tried to explain all that to Jayden, but Jayden seemed to take the refusal personally. Aegeus felt awful about the whole mess, but what was he supposed to do? It wasn't anything wrong with Jayden, it was something wrong with him, like always.

Why couldn't he be normal? Why couldn't he eat normal food, have normal sex, have a normal family? His original parents had probably recognized that there was something wrong with him, and that was why they'd abandoned him.

•————•————•

Dark thoughts circled in Aegeus's mind, thoughts that predicted failure, pain, even death. He was made all wrong, somehow, and no doubt that had caused the madness that was about to make him gut himself.

He couldn't stop, though. The scalpel was there, and with his eyes still fixed on it, Aegeus drove it into his own flesh.

There was a stab of pain, just as he'd expected, but the pain suddenly transmuted to something like relief. Aegeus gasped, then let out a low moan. Oh god, it felt so good, so satisfying, so exactly what he needed. Like picking off a scab when it was close enough to ready; a little bit of a sting, and yet so very *good*.

He drew the blade down slowly, carefully, his hand steady. He expected more pain, but got none at all. Instead the relief increased, as if every further inch he cut let out more of some impossible pressure.

There was almost no blood, either. A few drops beaded up along the scalpel's path, but surely the fact that he was cutting the full depth of the blade ought to have caused a lot more bleeding?

It didn't, though. There was just the thin red line. And, as he cut further and further, across the oddly shallow dimple of his navel—another little oddity, though at least one that had never bothered him—and down the lower curve of his belly, the sides began to split apart, revealing the layers of him, skin and fat and muscle all open to the air.

There was less fat than he'd expected, as if the distended softness of him was mostly innards. That seemed odd, since the rest of his body was certainly rounded and padded.

He almost wanted to reach inside, to feel what was there. There *was* something writhing, squirming, eager to be free within him; it hadn't been merely his imagination. But the single cut wasn't enough. What was in there would burst out through that narrow slice with too much force, he just knew it. It was holding back, waiting. *He* was holding it back somehow, tensing something. It felt like tensing his abs, but his abs weren't tensed—god, they were sliced apart! What was he doing? No, the muscles he was clenching were deep inside.

He found that little divot, and the tiny, nearly invisible furrow that began at that spot and traveled in a line across his belly. It had always been there, and he'd assumed it was a scar, something from infancy, but now, suddenly, he knew it wasn't. It was a seam. The seam from top to bottom followed the path a "happy trail" might take in an ordinary human, so he'd never remarked on it; but this perpendicular line was just as necessary for him, so it had been added to his human shape, somehow. He'd probably been born with it, he was sure of that at this moment. Just as he'd somehow been born with the seed of whatever strangeness was waiting to burst out of him. He'd been born strange, but as relief grew towards fulfillment, he knew that he wasn't made all wrong after all. He was made differently; made with something *more* than human.

Aegeus placed the scalpel's tip at the indent that was not a belly button at all, anticipation thrilling through him. He cut sideways, making a steady, sure, careful incision all along that fine, subtle line.

He moaned again as he did. *God* this felt so good. It wasn't sexual, not quite, but it was a deep, profound pleasure, coupled with an equally profound relief. Soon, soon, he'd be able to relax, to expand, to let that *more* inside him out.

The final cut was near bliss, following the narrow line across the other side of his belly, slicing everything open. There was a little blood from it all, right at the surface, as if he'd scratched his skin. Everything underneath was bloodless, meant to be cut, ready to open.

With hasty, eager fingers Aegeus set the scalpel back on the tray. It seemed he might not need the other things there at all.

Instead, he reached and pulled back the flaps of skin, laying himself open like some strange flower.

Then at last he relaxed and, like a flower, like a fern frond nudging up from the forest floor, he unfurled.

He had tentacles. This was his first thought as he looked at the thing blooming out of his belly. A dozen narrow, tapering things, each one perhaps a yard long, pinkish on their outer sides, duller and grayish on the inner sides, where rather than suckers they had little wrinkled ridges. They shone with slickness, and each was connected to the next by a membrane near its base, very like the way octopus arms were. In the middle of them, though, wasn't an octopus beak, but a pink, fleshy bud, with a furled, puckered orifice at its heart.

Aegeus stared in fascination, then reached down to touch. A tentacle reached back in what seemed to be an involuntary response, and curled around his hand. It felt slick, smooth, and warm. Its grip was strong too, like the unexpected narrow strength of a snake. He could feel through it, as he could through his hand, the soft skin of it sensing the touch of his fingers even as his fingers explored and touched the tentacle.

All the tentacles were moving and exploring, now, stroking and curling over his skin and over each other. When he tried to move them voluntarily they responded as readily as any other part of his body, but when he didn't consciously keep them still they seemed self-driven. Very like an octopus, he thought, which had extensions of its ring-shaped brain in each of its tentacles, so they thought for themselves.

Exploring further, he slid his hand down to the center of the tentacle-flower, to the pink bud there. As he touched it, a jolt of pure pleasure went through him, and an involuntary moan escaped him.

Oh, *fuck*. No wonder sex had always felt lackluster. He didn't need somebody to touch his cock, he needed *this*. He stroked his fingers over the surface of it, and moaned again. He was halfway there just from that. When he pushed a fingertip carefully inside, he came instantly with a soft, startled cry. His cock pulsed, a few thin spurts of seed coming from it, but his pleasure was definitely centered in the entrance at the heart of his tentacles, bliss radiating from where the little bud clenched rhythmically around his finger.

It began to ebb, but he couldn't resist moving his finger, pushing a little deeper, and with a groan Aegeus felt his pleasure beginning to build again.

"Oh . . . oh, yeah," he moaned. He lay back on the rug, closing his eyes, concentrating on sensation as he began to slowly finger the heart of his otherness. God, it was so perfect. Then it got even better when one of his own tentacles crawled between his legs, coiling around his cock. He hadn't meant to do it, but as soon as he realized what his half-conscious self had done, he continued deliberately, stroking his cock. What had been dull and insufficient alone was wonderful when added to the bliss of his finger in that tight, hot passage at his core.

Wanting more, Aegeus directed another tentacle lower, the slick tip of it breaching his anus, his own body a wonderful heat around the tentacle, the tentacle soon a satisfying fullness inside him as he pushed it deeper.

His moans trailed off into quiet, breathless gasps as he worked a second finger inside the little bud. It began to clench and pulse around his fingers, and with a groan of overwhelming bliss he came again. His cock barely leaked, the orgasm almost dry, but that didn't matter as his tentacles curled and thrashed and his back arched from the intensity of it.

When it was over he went limp, letting his hand fall. His tentacles relaxed, the one he'd pushed inside his backside withdrawing.

He floated in a warm haze, lying on the rug before the fire until the flames began to die down. For once he felt nothing wrong with him. No churning or pressure within, no nausea, no frustration or dissatisfaction. He was free, comfortable, and content, his tentacles curling slowly against each other, slick, warm, and wonderful, his body relaxed.

The dimming firelight eventually drew him to sit up with a low groan. He needed to stoke the fire, or else give up on it and turn on the lights. He stood, and stretched, stretching all his tentacles too with a happy sigh.

Thoughts of dinner led him to consider the fact that he needed to go shopping tomorrow, and indeed if he was to keep himself in fruit and firewood he would also have to go to work on Monday. Which meant he needed to be able to go out in public.

Experimentally, Aegeus tensed that inner muscle, happily finding he could pull his tentacles back inside. He smoothed down the flaps of skin and flesh with his hands, and smiled as they joined together, leaving only a cross-shaped pair of pink seams behind.

Having his tentacles coiled back inside again felt alright. It was like wearing a pair of pants that were a little too tight—not comfortable, exactly, but fine enough for a while. He'd be glad when he could stretch them, but he could keep them hidden if he needed to.

Smiling, he uncurled them again, his skin splitting open easily to let them out, and headed to the kitchen and the half-dozen apples waiting for him there.

It was good to be right, finally. He didn't know what he was, exactly—not human, probably—but whatever he was, he was himself, precisely as he should be, and it felt good.

Pinion and Thorn

*M*artin was in a hurry.

Of course he was *always* in a hurry; he didn't like to hold still, he didn't like to settle down, he didn't like to do any one thing or stay in any one place. But today's hurry was just the tiniest bit more urgent than usual.

Hooves pounding on the road behind him sent him diving for the bushes. He didn't watch; if he could see them, they could see him. So he didn't know if it was the city guard, the merchant's bondsmen, or some unrelated pair of people pushing their horses hard down the road.

So long as they didn't see him, it didn't matter.

When the sound of hoofbeats had passed out of hearing, Martin straightened and brushed his tunic off. He shrugged his shoulders, settling his pack into place, and was about to step back onto the road when he realized that he was standing on a different road from the one he'd dived off of.

It was old and overgrown—hence the bushes he'd hidden in—but there were no trees on it, and he could see, here and there, the remnants of ancient wagon-wheel ruts.

Well, why not? He had no destination in mind, no "towards" ahead of him, only an "away" behind him. If there was some ancient ruin out there, something that somebody had once thought important enough to build a road towards, and then abandoned, maybe there would be something there for him. At the least, there wouldn't be guards on his trail out there, so it'd be a good place to shelter tonight, assuming there was some kind of shelter.

So he set off down the old road, pushing shrubs out of his way now and again, and climbing over storm-felled trees.

The road meandered among the low hills for a time, then climbed, and eventually arrived at a manor house that sat on a hilltop, with a no-doubt beautiful view of the land all around. The manor was obviously long-abandoned, though, with greenery climbing its walls and rioting across its grounds.

As Martin drew closer to the gates, which stood gaping open, he saw that the greenery was entirely composed of rose bushes. They ran wild like brambles, nearly filling the space inside the crumbling stone walls that enclosed the grounds, while climbing vines wreathed the whole of the house. Flowers dotted it all, and the air was full of their heady scent.

"Wow," said Martin, looking at it.

Despite how overgrown it all was, though, the gravel path from the gates to the front door remained passable, so he walked slowly up it, looking around as he went.

The roses were a jumble of different kinds, showing every possible color a flower could be, and some that might be impossible. The house itself, though covered in vines, didn't seem to have fallen apart. The roof seemed sound, the walls still standing, none of it crumbling. Martin regarded the front door curiously. He set his hand on the latch, chuckled to find it was locked. The lock was still sound too, it seemed. His lock picks made short work of it, though. It was a decent lock, a little old-fashioned, but nothing special. The only reason it took more than ten seconds was the mechanism was stiff, probably rusted. The door squealed as it swung open, hinges obviously rusted too, and Martin stepped into the manor house's gloom with a delighted smile of anticipation on his face. What treasures and mysteries might lie here, waiting to be uncovered?

Inside everything was dim and . . . strange. He had expected a rotting ruin, with stained walls, broken by the vines growing everywhere.

Instead he found a neat, clean, tidy house, looking as if the owners had meticulously stowed everything away and then stepped out only a day or two ago. There was no rot, there was no mold, there was no dust, even. Only thorny vines crawling along the floor and sprouting up into bushes here and there.

Martin continued to explore, and things continued to be strange. There were roses pressing against the windows from the outside, and from the inside too, soaking up the light, yet all the windows seemed to be intact. Martin had the strange thought that the roses didn't want to mess anything up. Surely having plants grow everywhere ought to make a mess?

And where were the indoor roses coming from? The long vines running down halls and twining along baseboards had no sense of direction, they were simply everywhere. They had to be rooted outside somewhere, surely? He certainly saw no sign of them growing through the floor, only crawling along it.

Eventually Martin found himself in a room with a fireplace, and saw there was wood stacked in the woodbox beside it, and matches on the mantle. The exhaustion of a long, exciting day finally catching up with him, he made a fire, then rolled out his bedroll in front of it. The flames were pleasant against the late spring chill, and the prosaic nature of a hearth fire was a bulwark against the strangeness all around, including here, for rose stems writhed along the base of one wall, to where a bush grew lush against a window, dotted with crimson flowers.

The light outside was fading, the sun having set, and Martin scooted a little closer to the fire. The shifting light was probably the reason why, but he could almost swear a few of the rose vines moved closer too.

Whenever Martin felt uneasy, as he began to feel now, he had a tendency to babble. As he sat in front of the fire, he addressed the roses out loud.

"So, uh, roses? Do you like the fire? I didn't think plants would like fire. Wood is made of plants, right? I guess nobody burns rose bushes, though, so maybe you don't mind. You can't possibly be getting cold though, that would be silly. Nearly as silly as talking to a bunch of plants.

Who can't possibly hear me. But I just thought it looked like maybe you were cozying up to the fire? You're more than welcome to, I don't mind sharing. Just, er, don't like, strangle me in thorns or something? I've survived a lot of stuff in my life, so it would be pretty annoying to end things here because I was tired and went to sleep in the same room as a rose bush. I mean, can you imagine that on a tombstone? 'Wasn't wary of flowers.'" Martin laughed. He knew he was talking to himself; as weird as this place was, it wasn't like flowers had ears.

"I guess roses are the flowers a body should be wary of. I mean gosh, so many cliche stories about love and roses! Now if I was to come up with something interesting about flowers, I'd want to talk about crocuses." He halted and, feeling silly, added, "No offense! You're very pretty, and very magnificent! The biggest bunch of roses I ever saw! And the most interesting! So you're miles ahead of the kinds of roses in sappy love ballads, you know? I just also think crocuses are neat."

He yawned then. "Anyway, it's really late. You're completely fascinating, but I should probably have a bite and then sleep. Please, er, if you don't mind, don't strangle me in my sleep? I guess I could leave here, or try to barricade myself in some closet or something, but the fire is nice, and honestly I'm sure you're just plants. Really big, really weird plants, growing in a magic house, so who knows? But there's no way I'm moving on now, so . . . uh . . . just figured I'd ask. Thanks."

Martin pulled a round of hardtack and a chunk of salami from his pack, and swiftly devoured both, despite the amount of chewing required. Another yawn overcame him as he finished, and he curled up on top of his bedroll, the fire warming the room enough that he didn't need to climb beneath the blankets. A moment later he was deeply asleep.

* * *

Martin woke, feeling comfortably warm, with morning light filtering in around the rose bush in front of the window. He stretched and looked at the fire, then frowned. It was still burning, and the woodbox, which he'd barely touched the night before, was now empty. Huh.

As he looked around the room, another surprise struck him almost instantly. There was a plate sitting near the head of his bedroll, bearing a little heap of wild strawberries at the center of a nest of spring greens.

Martin blinked at this unlikely sight for a long moment. He was being served breakfast. By the house? By the roses? By something hidden or invisible that lived here, perhaps? Whatever it was, it didn't seem to keep food around, given that it had presented him with things that could be gathered from forest and field nearby. Still, it was a gift, and not to be scorned. "Thank you," he said to the empty air. "It's very kind of you to think of me."

He picked up one of the tiny berries and popped it into his mouth. It was sweet-tart, a perfect burst of flavor on his tongue, and he hummed in pleasure, then set about devouring the entire pile. It wasn't a meal, not even when he chewed on a few of the greens, faintly bittersweet and pleasant. It was good, though, and he felt strangely touched that whatever spirit or creature lurked here would be so considerate of his mere mortal needs.

Martin rolled up his bedroll and got it tied to his pack. Then he headed for the door, which he'd left unlocked and open, but found locked. This might be worrying, save for the fact that the lock was the kind one could twist open from the inside without a key. He did so and set out down the gravel path. "Thanks again," he called back to the house as he strode along, idly making plans to come back here and explore further, once his current business was done with.

About halfway along the gravel path, though, he caught a familiar glint from a flower bed deeper into the tangle of roses.

Gold.

"Huh." Martin looked at the bush, where the sun was definitely glinting off metal. And yet they were roses. They couldn't be made of real gold . . . could they?

He picked his way among the bushes, nimbly avoiding thorns. They blended together into one patch, but he could see where they had once been separate beds, so there were areas that were easier to pass through than others. He was scratched a few times, but made it to the particular bush that had golden roses without much trouble.

Martin reached out, and was shocked to find the metallic rose he touched did indeed feel like gold, stiff yet fragile, nothing like the soft yield of real rose petals. "Wow." He noticed that these roses were tiny, much smaller than the ones growing elsewhere, no doubt because of the weight of metal, which would bow the stems too much if they were larger. It had to be some kind of magic, and that meant he really *should* leave it alone, but Martin had never been good at "should."

He'd just take one. He wouldn't get greedy. Surely with a whole bush of these things the spirit of the place wouldn't mind just one?

Martin selected a rose that had just finished opening, young and beautiful, but with the full furl of its golden petals on display. He slid his hand down the stem and broke it off from the bush, preparing to tuck it into his belt.

Instead he yelped as there was a rumbling roar and the whole world seemed to shake around him. The vines around his feet grabbed him, tangling him, holding his boots tightly. He fell, but didn't hit the ground. Instead he hit more roses, thorny vines cradling his body, grasping at his clothes, wrapping him and binding him until he was utterly helpless. Martin thrashed instinctively for a moment, but the more he moved, the more thorns pierced him, so he went still, panting. "Fuck," he said, a shudder of terror going through him. "I'm sorry!"

There was a low growl, and then the vines began to carry Martin towards the manor house. "Oh fuck, oh fuck, oh fuck, look, I'm really sorry, I'll, uhm, I guess I can't put it back but really I didn't think just one rose would do any harm, you have so many and oh fuck, please don't kill me, please, please, please!" Martin couldn't help the terrified babble that spilled from his lips as the roses dragged him inside the house. They pulled him down the halls towards the kitchen and tossed him in an empty room full of shelves that had probably been a pantry.

Martin hit the floor rolling and got to his feet, prepared to make a break for it, but thorny vines covered the doorway almost entirely, twisting and writhing in agitation. One reached in, making Martin cower back, but all it did was pluck the gold rose out of his hand. Then it withdrew and the door slammed shut, leaving Martin in near-complete darkness. A rasping sound indicated a bolt being thrown, locking Martin in.

". . . okay then. Guess I'll . . . stay here for a while. Right." Feeling his legs shaking, Martin sat down on the cold stone floor. At least he wasn't dead. The lock had sounded like a deadbolt, so he probably couldn't pick it, but there were ways to jimmy those, so he might be able to get out. But the kitchen, all the halls, and the entire grounds were covered with roses, so he suspected getting out of the pantry would just result in him being put right back in it.

He sat there for a while, thinking, but couldn't come up with anything. Before long his eyes started to adjust to the dark. Light was leaking in under the door, which suggested the rose vines weren't covering it anymore. He was sure they were still out there, though. Unable to stay sitting any longer, Martin rose and paced the short length of his prison. Walking helped him think, but nothing came to him. How could he fight an entire estate full of apparently sentient plants? He couldn't. What weaknesses did plants even have? You could burn them, but past attempts to light fires in damp weather meant Martin knew perfectly well that wet wood didn't burn worth shit, and all those live, green rose bushes certainly weren't dry. Anyhow if he tried to burn them down before he was out of the house, he'd just kill himself. So that was out. You could hack vines apart, if you had an ax. He didn't have an ax, just a small knife. You could poison plants, but he didn't have poison and didn't know what was poison to plants, other than salt, but he certainly didn't have that, and anyway how would he even do that? He couldn't just fling salt on them in the house's halls, you had to salt the ground, right? So he'd have to get outside first, and have lots of salt, and probably wait a long time—weeks, months?—for it to work.

Nope, he was definitely stuck here.

"Well shit," muttered Martin, and flopped down with his back against the door.

After a while he said, "Hey, roses? Plant . . . person? People? I don't know. I really am sorry. I didn't know one rose would matter to you that much. That was awfully rude of me, I realize now, though. You were so nice, taking care of the fire and finding me breakfast and all that! I shouldn't have repaid your hospitality with theft. I mean, I won't claim to be a saint or anything, but I should know better than that. So I'm super sorry. I'm not just saying that because I don't want to be locked up here forever, though I'll be honest and say that's definitely a factor. But really, I am sorry. That gold rose was so pretty, though! I've never seen anything like it! Is it magic? Oh, uhm, I don't mean to pry or anything. Just rambling here. Nothing better to do. Uh . . ."

He drummed his fingers against the stone floor. "Yeah. If you keep me in here you're going to hear a lot of me, at least until I start dying of starvation or thirst or whatever. Sorry? I'm not very good at staying still and shutting up. I hope you don't mind. I guess if you do, you could let me go?"

Martin shifted, lying down and trying to peer out the crack beneath the door. He could see stone and a blur of green, and that was all. "Not bothered by the chit-chat, huh? Do you even have ears? I have no idea if you can hear me. I guess roses don't have ears? But roses also don't grow inside houses, especially not nice, tidy ones like this. Great job keeping the place up, by the way! Uhm. Where was I? Oh, right, roses. Roses generally can't pick people up, either. So maybe you can hear me? I'd be happy to pay you or do you some favors or whatever else, if you let me out? Really not looking forward to dying alone in the dark here."

Sitting up again, Martin wrapped his arms around his knees. That last bit of rambling had gotten a bit too real. He'd always been the sort to whistle in a graveyard, but the idea of being trapped in this tiny, black space, alone, until he died, was quite possibly the worst thing he could think of.

"Hey, uhm, I know I'm just some random thief. Nobody important. But you were so nice earlier. I think . . . I hope you maybe are a good rose . . . thing? Rose person?" Martin shivered, fighting back tears. "I just . . . I . . . I don't want to die, okay? And if you do want to kill me, maybe you could just . . . do it quick? I don't . . . I can't, really, I can't do this. I'm used to flying free, okay? I'm used to open space. I . . . I'm sorry. I'm so sorry. I didn't want to hurt you, I just thought the gold rose was pretty. I'm so sorry."

There was a rustling outside the door, and a grating, squealing sound, followed by a clank as the rusted bolt drew back. Then light flooded in, filtered by green leaves as vines pulled the door open.

"Oh, god. Thank you," said Martin, dashing out the door. He hardly even cared if the rose-creature had latched onto the idea of killing him swiftly or was going to let him go. He was just relieved to be out of that tiny, confining space.

He stood in the kitchen, looking around. Vines wove their way around the baseboards and bushes bloomed where the light fell, but additional vines were coiled in front of him, one of them lifting up, a rosebud at its tip like some kind of serpent's head.

"Uhm. So does this mean I can leave?"

The rose swung side to side.

"Oh. You want me to stay?"

The rose nodded.

Martin swallowed. "Okay. I guess if I'm not shut in a dark closet I'll take it. Sure. So . . . uh . . . now what?"

The rosebud didn't move, apparently having no better idea than Martin did.

"Uhm. You want me to stay here?"

The rose immediately nodded.

"Because . . . I stole your gold rose?"

The nod was emphatic, almost violent.

"Right. Okay. That's . . . not ideal from my point of view, but I'll happily take it. So, er . . . I guess I should go up to that room with the fireplace?"

The rose shook its . . . head? Was that a head?

"Oh? Where should I go, then?"

The rose made a sideways jerking motion, and moved across the room. Martin, still nervous but also fascinated, followed.

The rose led the way out of the kitchen, down a hall, up a flight of stairs, and to a bedroom. To Martin's surprise the room was furnished, and the bed didn't seem musty; it was fresh and soft when he prodded at it. "Oh. This is nice."

There was a desk there, with quills, inkwell, and paper, and a wardrobe, plus another open door that led to a small bathing room. Peeking in and seeing a tin tub, Martin was enraptured with the thought of a real bath. He turned back to the rosebud, which was waiting with an expectant air in the doorway. With a shock Martin realized there were no vines here, no bushes against the windows, nothing twining along the baseboards. There were roses on the outside of the windows, but inside the room was empty of them.

"I like this. Thank you, really. I'll stay here?"

The rose bobbed in an affirmative nod.

"But, uh, can I leave this room, too?"

The rose bobbed again.

"What about the house, can I go outside?"

The rose hesitated, then nodded slowly.

"Ah. Let me guess, then. I can't leave the grounds here?"

The rose nodded.

"Well, I guess that's fair. I violated your hospitality, so I'm your prisoner. I'm very grateful you'll let me have such comfortable quarters as this, though, and will let me roam the place as I please. That's kind of you."

The rose made an odd, wiggling sort of motion, as if it didn't know how to respond to that.

"You're a lovely sort of creature, you know. Made of flowers and so nice to me."

The rose turned away from him. It wasn't blushing, it couldn't, but was it . . . embarrassed?

"Er . . . okay, then. Uhm. You really are pretty, though."

The rose bobbed, then ducked out of the doorway, the vine retreating. Other vines were still running down the hall outside Martin's door, but none of those were flowering. He looked both ways and couldn't see any sign of the rosebud that had been communicating with him.

Martin shut the door and leaned against it for a long moment. Ordinarily he would have left it open, but he wasn't closing himself in, he was closing the roses out.

He investigated the room further for a while, but other than finding there were clothes in the wardrobe—fine-quality boy's clothes, near enough his own size, since he was on the short side for an adult, that he might wear some of them—he discovered nothing new.

From the room's window, though, he could see that there was a greenhouse amid the rose garden behind the house. It was one place he hadn't already explored, and as fear faded, boredom grew. Eventually Martin opened the door again. The vines looked just the way they had, and none of them reacted to his presence. So he slipped out the door and made his way through the house.

The back door turned out to be blocked by a thick tangle of climbing roses. Martin stared at them for a while, trying to decide what to do.

With a faint rustle, one of the flowers turned towards him. Deciding it couldn't hurt, Martin said, "Excuse me. If you don't mind, I'd love to go look around the back garden. I won't pick anything, I promise. Is there another back door, or should I go around from the front?"

The flower facing him tilted itself in a curiously thoughtful gesture, then with a louder rustling all the vines pulled back from the door, leaving it completely clear. The last one even helpfully lifted the latch and opened it.

"Oh! That's very obliging of you, thank you very much," said Martin.

The back garden was an even more disorderly tangle than the front, and some of the rose bushes here were nearly trees. Stems and branches blocked old paved paths, yet now they moved obligingly aside for Martin as he approached. He thanked them each time, wanting to stay in the good graces of whatever power commanded them.

Soon he reached the greenhouse. No vines climbed over it and no bushes came close to it, but its door was half open and the thick brown ropes of very old rose stems filled the lower part of the gap.

These did not move aside for Martin, but he was able to open the door further and carefully step over and around them.

Inside the greenhouse was warm and damp, as Martin had expected. It was full not of rose bushes nor of climbing vines, but of raised beds perhaps waist high, bearing small bushes and little sprouts.

Standing before one such bed, with his back to Martin, was a man.

Martin drew in a sharp, shocked breath, horrified, for the man seemed to be a prisoner of the roses in a much more profound way than Martin himself. Narrow vines coiled around his arms and legs while thicker ones wrapped about his hips. A fall of long, straight, silver hair obscured much of his back, with massive old vines vanishing under it, apparently wrapping his torso, and blooming flowers crowned his head. But then Martin noticed that the man's skin, utterly naked wherever the plant didn't cover it, was tinted green, and began to wonder. A moment later the man turned around, and Martin's eyes went wide in further shock. The rest of his body was leanly muscular, but his chest was skeletal, each rib bare of flesh, covered instead by vines and flowers that spilled out from his chest cavity.

His face was nearly skeletal, thin lips not quite hiding white teeth, nose barely there, cheeks sunken in, with a tiny pink rose blooming in one eye socket, while the other held an uncanny purple glow.

He was a horror, an awful blending of plant and man, and he was *beautiful*.

Silence stretched out between them as the rose man and Martin looked at each other. Aware suddenly that he was staring rudely, Martin cleared his throat. "Ah. Hello there. Sorry to intrude. I, uhm, I'm Martin. Er. Nice to meet you?"

The rose man opened his mouth, but all that came out was a low groan. And really, it was astonishing he could do that much, given he had flowers where his lungs should be.

"Oh. Ah. I'd ask your name, but I suppose you have no way to tell me. Uhm. I'm very sorry about that. I'm sure you're a wonderfully interesting person and all, and hey, my mother always said I talk enough for any two people, so I guess that balances out, but I'm unfortunately terribly curious and I wish I could ask you all kinds of questions, but—"

The rose man held up a hand, and Martin stopped his stream of nervous chatter. The man turned and moved towards one of the beds that held tiny seedlings. He didn't actually walk, Martin noticed. His feet, which were the gnarled brown of rose roots, hovered a few inches above the floor, while the thick vines that met his back, probably wrapped around his spine, carried him forward. He looked at Martin and beckoned with one hand.

Martin slowly approached. The man smoothed the bare dirt in front of the first row of little seedlings with his hand. Then with one finger he wrote in the smooth soil. *C-l-e-m-e-n-t.*

"Clement," said Martin. "Is that your name?"

The rose man nodded.

"It's a pleasure to meet you," said Martin, managing a smile. It was creepy, and strange, but he wasn't lying. He kept stealing glances at the rose man—at Clement—noticing more eerily beautiful details every time.

"Have you always lived here?" asked Martin.

Clement nodded.

"You, er, were born here, then?"

Clement nodded again. His hand smoothed away his name and he wrote, *My family home for generations.*

"Oh. I see. Uhm. And I take it you like roses?"

Clement made another groaning sound, but this time it was a broken-up, burbling thing. Martin realized he was laughing.

Roses are my life's work, he wrote in the dirt.

"You're alive then? No, wait, that's probably rude, sorry!"

Clement chuckled again. *I am alive*, he wrote.

"Ah, okay. I was just wondering, what with the skeleton look and all," said Martin.

The roses are alive, so I am alive.

Martin blinked. "Oh. You are the roses. So, ah, you're the one who, er, locked me up?"

I do not like having my self stolen, wrote Clement, his finger digging in deeper on "self."

"That makes complete and total sense," said Martin, nodding repeatedly. "I absolutely get you there, m'lord. If I'd known the rose was part of a person, I never would have picked it. I can't even imagine going up to somebody and just picking their hair, it would be beyond rude!"

Clement nodded curtly. *I have work to do now*, he wrote. Martin looked at the seedlings next to his words, seeing they had tiny flecks of gold in their leaves. Was he breeding gold roses? Martin didn't ask, though; he knew a dismissal when he read one.

"Right, m'lord! Though, ah . . ." Martin hesitated, then said, "It's getting to be dinner time. I can't just live on strawberries, either. You have any suggestions?"

Go to the kitchen, I will see what I can do, wrote Clement.

"Thanks!" chirped Martin. He turned to go, but couldn't resist looking back at the bizarrely beautiful man one more time before going out the door.

Martin thought about Clement as he went back into the manor house. There must be fairy magic involved here. No mere mortal could have created something like the melding of rose and human that so enthralled Martin.

He knew a little about fairy magic himself. He'd been told the story of his own christening many times, when a fairy woman who owed his mother a favor had appeared and blessed Martin with the swiftness to keep himself from harm. His father had sometimes joked that he should have asked the details, since they'd all thought the fairy would bless his feet, but obviously she'd actually blessed his tongue. And it was true that one way or another, with words or with swift feet, he'd always eventually gotten out of every bit of trouble he'd gotten into.

Martin didn't know if that would hold now, though. Clement's curse was obviously very powerful. It might negate Martin's blessing.

He arrived in the kitchen, where he found vines helpfully laying out a cast iron pan and several knives. One was curled around a cord of firewood, too, which it set by the stove. There was no sign of anything to cook yet, but Martin set about getting a fire built and the stove warming all the same.

He thought more about Clement's curse as he waited for the stove to heat and for whatever food might be provided him to arrive.

There were tales not unlike the situation he now found himself in. They usually featured a prince in a castle, not a minor lord in a manor, and a beautiful maiden, not a thief down on his luck, but still. In the tales the maiden would fall for the hideous but good-hearted monster, and her eventual declaration of love would break the curse.

Given that Martin thought Clement was anything but hideous, he figured he was already ahead of the game, if it was that kind of curse. Provided Clement proved to be good hearted, or at least able to tolerate Martin's constant babble, always the trouble he had with would-be lovers, Martin figured falling for him might not be very hard at all.

Martin was torn from this train of thought by a vine coming in the kitchen door, the limp body of a rabbit held in its coils. It appeared to have been strangled, which gave Martin a horrible shudder as he thought about how easily the roses could strangle him, but he pushed that aside as the vine deposited it on the kitchen counter and began to withdraw.

"Tell Clement thank you!" said Martin. "Or thank you Clement, if I guess you are the roses? This will be a very fine dinner!"

It wasn't as fine a dinner as it could have been, since he had no herbs, and no oil other than the meager grease of the rabbit's own fat. But he found a jar of salt, and that was enough to keep it from being tasteless, at least. He would have to ask about herbs later. Even if there was no herb garden, whatever patch had yielded the strawberries and wild greens might have wild onions, at least. For now, though, he was content to devour his dinner. He ate until he was stuffed, then stripped the remaining meat from the bones and wrapped it in a scrap of waxed paper he found in one of the kitchen's many cupboards.

He considered stowing his leftovers in the pantry, but found he wasn't willing to set foot there again, so settled for tucking the paper packet into a cupboard away from the stove, where it would stay cool during the night.

It was growing dark by then, so after banking the stove's fire, Martin took himself back to his room.

There were still no roses nor vines inside it, thankfully. He'd slept near them last night, but he hadn't known they were watching. There was no way he could sleep soundly now with the knowledge that Clement could probably see him somehow through the plants.

He bowed to one of the vines crawling along the hall outside and said, "Goodnight, Clement. I can't say I love being kept prisoner, but you've been more a host than a jailer, so I am very grateful. Sleep well, assuming you sleep, and I'll see you in the morning."

———•———•———•———

Morning came, and Martin woke with an awareness of being more than a little filthy. He was long overdue for a bath.

Fortunately, when he asked the vines in the hall, he soon had buckets of water being carried to the tub there by a surreal bucket brigade.

He found soap in a box on a shelf in the bathing room, and though the water was cold, he was more than happy to get clean. Once scrubbed and dried off with a towel from the same shelf, he dressed himself in clothes borrowed from the wardrobe. They weren't a perfect fit—he was short enough, but had broader shoulders than the boy they'd belonged to—but they were better than his own by-now-filthy things. He thanked the roses and Clement for the loan, then went to the kitchen, where he found the rabbit meat was indeed still cold, and that the roses had brought him three small, speckled eggs. So he stoked the fire and had a hearty breakfast.

After that he occupied himself for a while with a more thorough exploration of the manor house. For most of it he found nothing he hadn't seen before, but there was one door on the second floor that he hadn't noticed behind the roses covering it. They now obligingly moved aside for him, and inside he found a library.

The room had no windows, since sunlight might harm the valuable books, and it was small enough Martin left the door open beside him lest his claustrophobia overwhelm him, but the dozens and dozens of books there were an irresistible lure.

In other circumstances he would have assessed them by value first, to decide which of the heavy things to carry away and sell. But now he knew better than to steal from Clement. Even if a book wasn't as personal as a rose, his apologies would ring hollow if he made off with any of these now.

So instead he found himself perusing the titles for something to read, finding they were organized by subject in a neat and tidy fashion.

He ended up selecting a book of Roman mythology. Martin's name was Roman, though he'd never thought much of the connection. He felt he had more in common with Mercury, swift-footed god of thieves, than with Mars, god of war, but the subject seemed interesting. Clement, he thought suddenly, was a Roman name too, wasn't it? Perhaps he had something in common with his host and captor.

"I'm just borrowing this to read in my room," he said to the roses as he exited the library, the other place where none of them grew. They were probably bad for the books.

A nearby flower nodded permission, so Martin carried the book back to his room, and passed a few hours there reading.

The stories were fascinating, but filled with more tragic bad endings than he liked. What if he and Clement were somehow doomed by their names to be in a similar tragedy? He hoped not. Though if he was going by names, Clement at least meant something good. Martin wanted the sort of story he'd been raised with, where however bad things might get, the end would eventually be a happily ever after. The story with the cursed prince and the maiden held prisoner ended like that. Martin hoped his own situation was a parallel to that tale, and not to the older, sadder ones.

Setting the book aside, Martin rose and paced the length of the room a few times.

He didn't know what to do with himself now. It was hardly past noon, judging by the angle of the sun, hours yet until it would be time to make dinner. He didn't want to merely sit and read, but what else could he do?

Finally he went out into the hall. "Hey, Clement, m'lord. I hope it's okay to call you lord? I have no idea what your proper title is, but at least I'm saying you're in charge around here, right? Anyway, I gotta admit I'm used to being on the move, and having company." A rose had turned towards him by now, hopefully indicating Clement was listening. "Don't get me wrong, I don't want to be clingy or anything, but I like conversation, you know? I get you're probably busy, but it would be great if we could chat a little. I'd be happy to hang out in the greenhouse while you work, I wouldn't touch anything, I'd just talk. What do you say?"

The rose didn't move for a long time, and Martin's stomach sank. "Hey, it's okay if you don't have time . . ."

Then the rose shook back and forth once, bobbed up and down twice, and moved down the hall, pausing to turn back to Martin when he didn't immediately follow.

"I can come along?" he asked, and the rose nodded.

Feeling strangely delighted, Martin followed the rose to the back door. It stopped there, but the nod towards the greenhouse was enough to tell Martin where to go.

Clement was tending the seedlings, just as he'd been before, and just as before he was inhumanly beautiful. "Hey there, m'lord," said Martin cheerfully. "Hope I'm not interrupting anything too important. Maybe you could tell me what you're doing in here? I'd be happy to help if I can."

Turning away from the bed he'd been tending, Clement let out another low groan. A vine from his arm uncoiled and reached under one of the beds, coming out with a flat, rectangular object. Out of context, Martin didn't immediately recognize it, but when Clement put a stick of chalk to it and began writing, he realized it was a slate tablet, the kind used to teach children their letters.

"Oh! Wow, you got something so you can talk to me? That's amazing! Thank you."

Clement made a grumbling sound and turned the tablet to face Martin.

You can help water the young ones, if you like, it said.

"Sure thing, m'lord. Just show me what to do."

It was an easy enough task, once he knew where the water barrel and watering can were. He soaked each little seedling and small bush, making sure the soil was wet but not completely waterlogged. He chattered all the while, unable to help spilling nearly every thought that passed through his head out his lips. Clement mostly didn't respond, but every now and then he would chalk some reply, which delighted Martin beyond measure.

He wasn't being ignored and he wasn't being told to shut up; Clement was listening, and didn't seem to mind the babble.

"So what are you doing here?" asked Martin eventually. "Breeding new kinds of roses?"

Clement groaned in a positive sort of way and nodded. He chalked on his slate, *I always have, even when I was young.*

"Wow. When I was young mostly I just bothered my siblings and caused trouble. That's great! Is there a particular goal you're working towards?"

Two goals, wrote Clement. *One is very close, the gold rose bush. I already have the flowers, as you know.*

"Oh yeah. They're amazing. I'm sorry for stealing one, but come on, can you blame me? I'd never seen anything like them!"

Clement actually smiled, his thin lips turning up at the corners. It made him look even more skull-like, but Martin still didn't find it unpleasant.

The other is the true black rose, and that is much harder.

"Huh. I would have thought the gold harder, but I'm hardly an expert on roses," said Martin.

The plants take up the metal, if you provide it in the right form, scratched Clement's chalk across the slate. *It requires only a small touch of magic for the flowers. The full plant is harder, for the green is what gives plants life.* He erased that and kept writing, apparently enthused about explaining. *There is no natural black flower, though. So I must work to encourage an unnatural thing.* He wiped that off and added, *Shall I show you my best attempt so far?*

"Sure thing, m'lord. I'd love to see that!"

Clement, still smiling that skeletal smile, nodded and beckoned, gliding out of the greenhouse. Martin followed, not nearly as curious about the flower itself as about its creator.

The flower in question proved to be in the front yard. The roses there all seemed smaller, younger. The riot of colors Martin had first noticed were no doubt developed by Clement himself. Clement led the way, his vines carrying him, to a small bush covered in velvety black flowers.

Martin stared at them. The leaves were ordinary green, but the flowers were incredibly dark, showing stark against them.

"Wow, m'lord. I thought you said you didn't have any black roses yet. These look pretty black to me!"

Clement shook his head and cupped his hand around a flower, one that was fully open, petals almost flat. He groaned again, the sound seeming to carry some meaning. Martin stared at the rose and realized that it wasn't truly black. The heart of it showed dark red, and the petals were actually a deep, deep maroon. They looked darker on the buds and half-opened blooms, but they weren't actually black at all.

"Oh. I see, boss. I gotta say, though, that these are beautiful. I've never seen anything like them. True black or not, I bet folks would pay a ton to have roses like these."

Clement grumbled, a deep sound of annoyance. Martin ventured a guess. "Not interested in what people will pay for, m'lord?"

At Clement's nod Martin continued. "That's understandable. You're a lord and somebody important. Me, though, I've always been a poor nobody, so it's hard to not think about making my fortune."

Martin shrugged with a smile. "Guess for now my fortune is here with you."

Clement looked at Martin, and his expression seemed confused. Martin wished he'd thought to grab the slate before they'd left, but all he could do now was say, "That's not a complaint, I like your company fine. I could be doing a lot worse. Lotta poor folks do."

Clement grumbled, frowning, but then nodded. He beckoned and Martin followed him back to the greenhouse. Clement picked up the slate there and scrawled, *You could make a fortune with roses?*

"Maybe, m'lord. I'd need a good bit of luck, since I don't know a lot about them, but if I could find the right partner, or the right buyer, probably, yeah."

Is that why you came here, to make your fortune?

Martin laughed. "Oh hell no. I came here because I was running for my life after a con gone wrong and I figured nobody would look for me in some crumbling old mansion."

I see. Clement wiped the slate clean after that and turned away from Martin.

"Uh . . . m'lord?"

Clement picked up the chalk again and wrote, *Dinner will come soon, my vines are hunting. Go now, please.*

"Okay. Hope I haven't bothered you. If you want to throw me out on my ear, you can, and I'll be happy enough to be free, but . . ." Martin hesitated, then spoke nothing but truth when he said, "If you want me to stay, being here isn't a hardship."

Clement gave him a long look, then nodded and gestured to the door with no further reply. Martin thought, as he walked back to the house, that if he really was living in the fairy tale of the cursed beast, he was doing well, because the more time he spent with Clement, the more he liked him.

———————•———•———•———————

Martin needed to run.

Over the past few weeks at the manor, he'd done well. He'd chattered and read and helped out day after day. He almost loved Clement, even, but it had finally become too much. He couldn't endure sitting, reading, talking, doing nothing more active than watering plants for one single moment more. He knew Clement would never let him go, and if he'd been some other type of person, that might not have bothered him, for he really did like the strange man. But he was himself, and he had to do something, else he would go mad.

He went to the front gardens, where the paths weren't too overgrown, and began to jog along them, circling the rose bushes in convoluted loops. The jog turned to a trot, to a run, to a flat-out sprint that continued until Martin had to slow to a walk while he caught his breath.

He halted for a moment, leaning against the wall beside the front gate. It was open, as it had been when he'd arrived. The roses would stop him if he tried to leave. Surely the roses would stop him. But did he know that if he'd never tried? Maybe he could go just a little bit beyond the gate? Maybe he could pretend it was possible to fly free? He was a prisoner, but he could imagine . . .

The sound of hooves crunching on gravel froze Martin in place.

A voice from far too close said, "This is stupid, he's not going to be here after all this time."

Another said, "He's not been through Antriyh, and there's no forks in the road, so he's either gone this way or gone into the woods to get eaten by wolves."

Heart pounding, Martin hesitated. If he looked around the corner, well, he knew perfectly well that anybody he could see would be able to see him in return. But he *had* to know how many there were, how bad it was. He took a quick peek out the gate, heart pounding. There were four men on horseback. One he could have probably taken, two might be possible with luck, but four?

Then one of them shouted and spurred his horse forward. Martin, his mind a frantic jumble of curses, gave up on hiding and raced for the manor house. At least inside the men after him would be off their horses.

He didn't get that far, though, before the hoofbeats were on him. Martin half expected to simply be trampled, but instead he was grabbed by the back of his tunic and hoisted up into the air. "There you are, you slippery little bastard," growled the man holding him. Martin elbowed the man as hard as he could, but his captor knew what he was doing, and Martin was shoved facedown over the horse, left without any leverage, without a chance to do any real damage.

The other horses whinnied and jostled as the man shouted that he'd gotten the thief and his fellows all pulled up and turned about.

They began moving towards the gate, Martin struggling and kicking frantically as they went. He knew the only reason they hadn't killed him already was so they could have the spectacle of a hanging once they got him to town. He had to get loose somehow, anyhow, or he'd be dead by sundown tomorrow. Nothing he did accomplished anything, though.

Just as he was starting to panic, there was an equine scream, followed by yelling and cursing. The horse whose withers Martin had been thrown over half-reared, letting out a high-pitched neigh. Martin grunted as it thudded back to all fours, and tried to see what was going on. The scene was chaotic, but it was instantly obvious that though the wrought iron gates were still standing open, the exit was closed, for roses completely choked the space between the garden walls. Not only that, but they were writhing forward, reaching for the horses' legs and lifting to claw at the riders too.

Martin saw his chance and yanked from his captors' grip to tumble off the horse. He expected to land hard on the gravel path, but instead was caught by the roses, a dozen narrow green vines with hardly any thorns lowering him unharmed to the ground.

Even as he got to his feet, Martin heard a deep, angry roar, followed by screams, not just from horses, but from men. He looked up and saw Clement, his vines lifting him high above the ground, the lesser ones extended and lashing about him, a figure of terrifying beauty and deadly violence, which descended on the quartet of thief-takers. The maddened horses fled, heedless of their riders, who mostly seemed eager to be gone themselves, though their leader shouted defiance as his animal bore him away with the rest.

The vines blocking the gate were suddenly nowhere to be seen, and the four terrified horses and three terrified riders—and one angry, defiant rider—dashed through them into the forest beyond. Then the vines closed in again, blocking the exit completely.

Martin hardly saw that, though. He flung himself at Clement, trembling with the knowledge of how close to death he'd come, and hugged his rescuer—and captor—tightly.

"Oh god, Clement, you saved me. Thank you, thank you, you are so wonderful. I love you."

He hadn't meant to say it. He hadn't thought he was ready to try to break the curse. But it burst from him all the same, and once he realized what he'd said, Martin found himself braced for some change, some whirl of magic, something that would release Clement from his roses and return him to the conventionally handsome man he must surely have been.

There was nothing, though—only the strange feeling of Clement's cool flesh in Martin's arms.

Martin let go and cleared his throat. "Ah, sorry, m'lord, guess I got ahead of myself there. Didn't mean to declare eternal love or anything. Just, uh . . . well . . ."

Clement frowned, then beckoned to him, and Martin followed him around the manor to the greenhouse, where he retrieved his slate and chalk.

Why say love? he wrote, his chalk pushing so hard against the slate that he broke the stick in half. Martin looked up at Clement's face and shivered at the hard, angry expression there. *Is this a trick, am I one of your cons?*

"No, my lord, I swear it," said Martin sadly, looking away from Clement. He would never be free, and he would now suffer the torment of his only company being someone he loved who would never love him back. "I've never lied to you," he added. "At first I didn't dare and then I didn't want to. But I'm sorry, really I am."

You have lied, scrawled Clement, with swift, sloppy strokes. *You said you loved me. That has to be a lie!*

"It's not, really it's not. I know it's pretty fast and I know you don't like me at all and I'm sure I just annoy you like I do everyone. I do love you, but I'll try to give you more space."

Clement stared at Martin for a long time. He erased the mess of his previous words on the slate. Then he slowly wrote, *No lies. Swear again that it's true. You love me?*

Martin swallowed and said, miserably, "I swear. I do, yeah."

Clement turned the slate so that Martin couldn't see what he wrote next. He was being slow and careful, but whatever it was wasn't long, so only a moment later he turned the slate back.

Martin stared at the words there, stunned into silence.

I love you too, it said.

"R-really?" breathed out Martin, looking up at Clement. He nodded, a small, strange, but warm smile on his face. Then he dropped the slate onto the nearest flower bed and stepped forward to fold Martin in his arms. The embrace was as bizarre as everything else about Clement, since his arms were cold and the chest Martin was pressed to was all bone and flowers, not to mention the way the rose stems were studded with thorns. As Clement tipped his head down, though, and Martin went up on his toes and tipped his own head back, he wasn't bothered one bit by any of it. All he knew was the cool press of Clement's thin lips to his as they kissed, the way Clement opened to Martin's questing tongue, and the taste of him—roses, of course, roses and sweetness—as they kissed deeply, lingeringly.

When they finally broke apart Martin was breathless with it. He was also, though, once again braced for that swirl of magic. Yet once again nothing happened.

"Huh."

Clement tipped his head to the side and made a questioning sound.

"I kinda expected us both declaring love to break your curse, like it does in all the stories," he said.

Clement looked at him for a moment, his expression startled. Then he chuckled, which swiftly grew into a full laugh.

"Uh . . . my lord?"

One of his vines dropped the slate and chalk into Clement's hands, and he wrote, *It's not a curse.*

"Huh? But . . ." Martin gestured at everything helplessly.

Clement laughed again. *It may have been meant as a curse. I was afraid, when I was young and I first found my roses growing within me.* He put one hand over his chest for a moment, still smiling that faint skull's smile. *But I soon came to like it. It's not a curse.*

"Oh. I'm just as glad, then!" Martin found himself laughing too. "I'm sure you were a very handsome human, but you are *gorgeous* the way you are now. I thought breaking a curse on you would be worth it, but I'd miss how amazing you are like this."

Clement looked startled. Martin thought he would have been blinking in surprise if he could have, but he didn't seem able to blink. *I'm terrifying*, he wrote. *People scream and run away.*

"You sure are, m'lord! But they're not mutually exclusive, you know. You're terrifying and you're terrifyingly beautiful. I could just look at you all day."

The high arch of Clement's cheeks turned a golden bronze, and Martin grinned, realizing delightedly that Clement was blushing. He reached up and cupped Clement's face in one hand, stroking his thumb over the blush. "You're the most beautiful person I've ever seen," he murmured, and then kissed Clement again.

◆　　◆　　◆

Fresh out of the bath and wrapped in a towel, Martin stood at the window, looking out at the greenhouse. There were no signs of movement there, though from this distance he'd hardly be able to see any, especially not with the massive rose bushes in between.

Clement must still be out there. After saving Martin the day before, he'd said—or rather written—that they should talk more soon, but he'd wanted to tend to the roses that might have been damaged by their attack on the invaders first.

His roses had delivered more eggs this morning for breakfast, and had brought water for his bath, but Martin hadn't seen Clement himself all day.

A knock on the door made him jump and spin around. Who the hell could be knocking here? It had to be Clement. Probably. Hopefully.

The knock came again, a gentle tapping that might be one of the roses, it was so soft. Letting out some of his tension in a long breath, Martin crossed the room and cracked the door open.

Clement himself was standing on the other side. Though his feet were still not touching the ground, the wrist-thick vines that supported him curled and coiled along the hall.

"Oh! Ah. Come in?"

Clement gave Martin an up-and-down look, followed by a skull-like smile. He scrawled something on his slate and turned it around. *Should I come back once you're dressed?*

"If it bothers you. I've never been shy." Martin grinned. "Anyhow, it's not like you wear clothes at all."

Clement made that hiccuping groan that passed for a laugh and chalked, *I have leaves to keep me decent.*

Martin chuckled. "And I'm wearing a towel." He stepped back from the door. "Come in if you like."

Clement nodded and moved into the room. He hesitated in the middle of it, while Martin plopped down to sit on the bed. He patted the spot beside him. "Have a seat. Er, assuming you can, m'lord?"

Clement went to the bed, his expression thoughtful. Then he nodded and turned around, the vines that supported him partially crawling up onto the bed, before sitting down there with an audible creak of bending wood from his knees.

"So. Ah. Talking. You know I'm great at that! Guess we've got a lot we could talk about now? You wanna start anywhere in particular? If you don't, I've got approximately five thousand questions for you."

Clement chuckled, a low, wheezing noise. He wiped off the slate, then scrawled, *Many questions here too, but one first. Why my lord?*

Martin laughed, feeling his cheeks heat. "Well, it's a joke, mostly. Can't stand it when people lord it over me, see? So I took to calling everybody m'lord and m'lady. Beggars, serving girls, kings, whatever. They all get the same. That way when some pompous twit who could probably have me whipped for insolence insists I give him respect, I can laugh to myself, because he doesn't know I'd call the stableboys the same, you see?"

I see.

"So can I ask one now? Shall we trade back and forth?"

Clement smiled and nodded.

"Whose room is this? Somebody important, seems like, since the roses don't go here."

Clement looked around the room for a moment, cleaned the previous words off the slate slowly, then wrote in an equally slow, careful hand, *It was mine.*

"Damn." Martin looked at Clement, who even sitting was nearly a head taller than he was, and whose green-fleshed but broad shoulders would more than tear the seams out of the tunics that were only a hair snug on Martin. If these clothes had been his . . . "You were awfully young when you stopped living here, then."

I was 15, he wrote. *And if you want to know more . . .*

Martin smiled on seeing Clement write out the ellipsis rather than merely stop writing. But while he made the three little dots, a coil of his vines reached over his shoulder and dropped a sheaf of papers atop the slate. Clement gathered them in his hands, squaring them up neatly, then held them out to Martin.

"Oh. This is your story? How the flowers happened?"

Clement nodded.

Martin took the papers, smiling down at them. "That's quite a gift, sir. Really it is. I'm not a fast reader, though. I love stories, but it's hard to sit still for letters, you know? I'd rather talk to you for a bit, and save this for later, if that's okay?"

Clement nodded again, his smile returning.

Martin put his hand over Clement's, where it rested on the bed, chalk loosely held in it. Clement started, then relaxed.

Martin stroked over the back of it, feeling how it was nearly like a normal man's, with all the same tendons and muscles, yet it was cool, as cool as the air outside, and the flesh was pale and greenish. Martin eventually couldn't resist, so he lifted it to his lips and kissed the knuckles. "When I call you my lord, it's only a little bit of a joke, you know. I've got a hell of a lot of respect for you. Among other things."

Clement looked at Martin, his expression uncertain. He gently tugged his hand back so he could write. *I still don't understand it. I love being as I am, but no one else has ever loved me this way.*

"What can I say? I like new things. I like exciting things. And I never have fit in anywhere, so somebody else who doesn't either . . . that seems okay to me. Mostly, though, I mean hell, roses are the standard for beauty, you know? Guys write poetry comparing fancy ladies to them. You're *beautiful*, that's just all there is to it."

Thank you, wrote Clement, and Martin smiled to see that his cheeks were turning bronze again as he blushed. Then under it, *You're handsome yourself. And good to me like no one else.* He rubbed that out and added, *You can leave. I can't justify keeping you over a single rose, after coming to know you. But you can stay too.*

"God, Clement, my lord . . . thank you. I get a little stir-crazy being stuck standing still. I *will* go. I gotta fly free. But, well, I'll come back, whenever I go. I think this is home now. Right now, in fact, I don't want to be anywhere but here." He shifted, turning to Clement, going up on one knee on the bed. He put a hand to Clement's sunken cheek and urged his head around. Clement responded, and a moment later they were kissing again.

Clement's lips were hardly there, Martin could feel his teeth, and when he slipped his tongue in to explore, Clement was cool, his own tongue nearly dry, but tasting of roses and nectar. Martin hummed with pleasure and kissed more, letting his hands wander over Clement's cool skin. Some places he was skeletal and some places he wasn't. The vines only seemed to sprout along his spine, though they coiled and curled everywhere, especially around his hips—as he'd said, the leaves kept him decent. Martin was very curious, though, about what might be under those leaves.

He considered letting his hands wander there, but before he could, Clement put his own hands on Martin's hips, their cool, strong touch making him shiver, even through the towel. It wasn't the temperature doing it, after all, it was everything, including the thought of what might come next.

"Just so you know, my lord, I'm a really flexible guy, and I'm up for whatever here. You just lemme know if I go too far, okay? I'll do the same."

Clement nodded and shifted his hands higher, touching bare skin along Martin's sides. His caress was tentative, cool fingers brushing lightly, slowly exploring Martin. Martin hummed in pleasure, holding back the urge to give verbal encouragement. He knew he talked too much and knew chatter during intimacy put a lot of lovers off.

The hum did seem to urge Clement on, though, for he moved his hands further, daring to explore more, thumbing over one of Martin's nipples.

"Oh, yeah, that's good," said Martin, unable to keep quiet at that. He loved having his nipples played with. He knew not all guys did, but it was one of his favorite bits of foreplay.

Clement rubbed the other nipple as well, circling and pressing on both little nubs for a moment. Then he paused, his expression turning to a frown, as much as it could with his skeletal features, and he lifted his hands away with a low groan Martin couldn't interpret.

"Clem? You don't have to do anything you don't want to, just 'cause I like it."

Clement huffed, which for a moment made Martin worry he'd said or done something wrong. Then he snatched up his slate and scrawled on it. *I want to do what you like.* The chalk hovered hesitantly over the slate, then Clement added, *I don't know what to do, though.*

Martin blinked at Clement for a moment, puzzled. Then the pieces fell into place. He'd turned into a flower-monster when he was 15. He'd acted like nobody had ever found him beautiful that way. So he'd probably never had a lover at all.

"Oh wow, m'lord. No, no, don't worry about that. I'll be happy to give you some pointers. If you don't mind my chatter while we're doing things? But I'm easy to please, really I am."

Clement dropped the slate and chalk, and nodded.

"Okay. So, to be honest, my lord, the thing I want most right now is to get to touch and explore every single inch of you. If you're not okay with that, I don't mind, but damn, you're just so incredible! And maybe if you lie back and I do the work, that'd be easier to start with? What do you think?"

That got another nod from Clement, which had Martin grinning in return, and very much aware that his cock was starting to stand up beneath the towel.

"Great! Can you lie down on the bed, m'lord?"

Clement stretched out on his back, vines and leaves shifting all around him. His hips were still covered in concealing leaves, but the vines uncoiled from much of the rest of him, leaving him open to Martin's roving gaze, which was immediately followed by Martin's fingers. He traced over soft, cool skin that seemed to cover muscles and tendons just like anyone's, and over the spots where flowers had torn through, showing Clement's hollow chest, bones stark and pale, the dark vines that emerged between them contrasting sharply, all of it dotted with flowers in various states of bloom.

Martin touched some of those too, and when he bent to press a kiss to the hollow of Clement's neck, he was surrounded by their scent.

Clement made a soft sound, almost a gasp, when Martin did that. Martin glanced up. It was hard to read Clement's expression, but he didn't look displeased, so Martin continued, tracing a line of kisses down the center of Clement's chest, lips pressing to cool, smooth bone wherever it showed among the flowers.

"Haaa . . ." The breathy groan was definitely a sound of pleasure, so Martin continued, sprinkling kisses along Clement's abdomen, which seemed to be mostly normal flesh, though a little vine tip poked out of it a hand's-breadth to one side of his navel. Martin kissed that too, on impulse, and the gentle sigh from Clement suggested he could feel it.

That was an interesting thought, but Martin would explore how much the roses could feel later; right now he was intent on exploring something else.

There was a thin trail of silvery hair running from Clement's navel down to vanish among the leaves, and Martin slowly, deliberately kissed along that line, letting his kisses grow open-mouthed, and adding in nips now and then.

Clement groaned softly, and some of the vines around him began squirming and writhing. Martin thought that might be a good sign. He was sure of it when the ones keeping Clement "decent" began to move too, pulling slowly back as Martin kissed his way down.

At first they didn't reveal much, only more pale, greenish skin sprinkled with white hairs, but eventually the slow retreat bared a half-hard cock, as green as the rest of Clement, but seeming ordinary other than that.

"Well now, that's just lovely." Martin put a final kiss on the shaft of Clement's cock, then stroked his fingers along it, unable to help a hum of satisfaction as it hardened in his hand.

"Haa. Ahhhh . . ." The soft sounds were still encouraging, and Clement's cock looked more than enticing, the head beginning to turn that golden-bronze color. A bead of something that was also golden, like honey, welled up at the tip of it, and Martin couldn't possibly resist that. He dove down and lapped it up, tonguing broadly across the tip of Clement's cock.

It tasted entirely unlike either pre or cum. It had a complicated flavor—bitter, floral, sweet, and resinous all at once. Martin thought it might be sap, but whatever it was he didn't mind it in the least.

Clement made a sound something like a gasp, then another of those low, breathy moans as Martin took the head of Clement's cock between his lips and began to go down on it.

Martin couldn't describe the sound Clement made at that; it was a groan and a creaking, and something almost like a whimper. But the way his hips jerked up, driving his cock deeper into Martin's mouth, Martin was certain Clement was enjoying things, if with a certain inexperienced enthusiasm. Fortunately Martin was very good at this. He loved sucking cock or eating somebody out, and had long since learned to completely suppress his gag reflex. Clement's hands gripped the blankets and his vines coiled and writhed, clutching and stroking at Martin, somehow without the thorns touching him. His hips kept bucking too, no doubt moving on instinct, but Martin loved the enthusiasm, opening his throat and letting Clement fuck into it.

It was fantastic, but the hard ache of Martin's own cock made him consider other alternatives, and when a thought flitted through his head he pulled back, glad that Clement let him, since if he'd wanted he certainly could have held Martin down.

"Fuck, Clem, you have no idea how hot you are," said Martin breathlessly, looking up at Clement.

Clement was propped on his elbows, his chest moving as if he were breathing, little huffs coming from him somehow, his eyelids completely wide open, the dim glow on the one side a bright pinprick now, the other empty at the moment, yet giving the impression of staring at Martin.

Martin crawled up, leaving his towel behind to straddle Clement, feeling vines and leaves embrace his legs. The ache of his cock brushed against the cool hardness of Clement's, and Martin moaned softly. "Oh, yeah. Oh, fuck. Yeah." He shifted, rubbing his cock along Clement's length. They were much of a size, even if different in so many other ways.

Clement dropped back, no longer propped up to watch, his head tipped back as he groaned in pleasure.

With a groan of his own, Martin curled his hand around both their cocks, squeezing them together. Clement shivered, all his vines moving again, and bucked his hips up. Martin moved with him, rubbing their cocks together, stroking them, smearing pre and sap over both.

"Ah, yeah, Clem . . . fuck . . ." Martin was panting fast, pleasure racing through him. Just as good, though, was the sight of Clement laid out beneath him in all his uncanny beauty. He had one hand partially over his face, as if embarrassed to be seen, and Martin almost wanted to reach out and pull it off, to tell Clement not to cover himself, but maybe that would be too much. And anyhow, the rest of him was very much on display, his body framed in vines and flowers.

The groan of pure bliss Clement let out was more than amazing, too, even with his face half-covered, and so was the way he tensed, bucking into Martin's hand, against Martin's hard, hot cock. He had to be close.

"Come on, Clem. Please. I want to see you come. Come for me."

"Haah!" Clement shuddered beneath him, and a moment later his cock was pulsing in Martin's hand, spurting thick, honey-golden fluid over his belly and chest, drops of it spattering the petals of his roses like dew.

"Fuck," gasped Martin. He didn't have words for how seeing the gorgeous, unreal man beneath him come in his hand made him feel. He moaned as he continued to stroke their cocks together, milking every drop from Clement. When the last pulse was done, Martin gave Clement's cock one more soft caress, then gripped his own all the tighter. "God, what you do to me," he breathed, stroking himself rapidly, not wanting to hold back a second longer. "God, Clem, yes!"

He came in a rush of pleasure, pearly white joining the honey-gold decorating Clement.

When he'd come down from the rush of climax, Martin couldn't resist lifting his well-stained hand and tasting the mixture of herbal bittersweetness and ordinary salt and musk on it. He sighed deeply and smiled down at Clement. "Damn, my lord. You are amazing. It's going to be a while before I'm tempted to leave, assuming I get to do this now and then."

Clement looked up at Martin, his natural skull-like smile widening, the rest of his expression softening. He reached up and cupped Martin's cheek. Martin nuzzled into that caress, and was more than happy to cooperate when Clement pulled him down and around to lie alongside. Martin pillowed his head on Clement's shoulder and stroked Clement's hair, feeling the delicate stems woven through the roots of it, supporting the crown of roses atop his head. Meanwhile the vines gently curled around them both, covering Clement's hips again, and cradling Martin, still somehow without more than the faintest prick of thorns.

With a happy sigh Martin said, "Yeah, think this might just work out, my lord. I'm madly in love, you're beautiful and amazing and— even more madly—you somehow love me too. Curse or no, it looks like we might get our fairy-tale happily-ever-after anyway."

Clement made a soft noise that sounded pleased. He could have gotten the slate and said something, but he seemed happy to merely indicate his agreement and seal that with a soft, rose-sweet kiss.

The Lighthouse Keeper

*O*n the western horizon the moon was setting into the sea. It was a peaceful night, the sky clear and star-strewn above, the ocean quiet, waves coming in to roll across the sand with a soft, repeated susurration. Dunes climbed from the shore, dotted with scattered tufts of beach grass on the seaward side, the landward side beginning to grow brambles and other bushes. Those blended into the undergrowth of the forest beyond, pine trees casting long, inky shadows that soon concealed all.

Amid those shadows there was a low laugh, followed by a breathless giggle. Other sounds followed, soft but unmistakable: the sounds of two young lovers, stealing a moment away from older eyes.

They were hidden in the shadows, the young woman with her back against an outcropping of stone, where the bones of the land showed through the verdant green, the young man pressing her to it, hands roaming, disarranging her clothing.

Soft moans and murmured words were interrupted by another sound, a rushing overhead, as if a gust of wind had suddenly come up from nowhere, and a thrashing in the pines as something pushed down among the branches, making them whip and creak.

The lovers froze, both looking towards the sound, neither able to see anything in the increasing dark, even the moonlight nearly gone now as the sea consumed it.

A harsh scraping, grating sound came next, like a cat using a scratching post but a hundred times louder. The young woman let out a shriek and the sound instantly halted. A shadow—deeper black against the night—turned towards them, its eyes lit with a ghostly purple glow. Three of them, arranged in a triangle, pupils broad and black in the darkness. They were huge, the size of a man's fist, and were at twice a tall man's height, easily. Something gaped open beneath them, showing sharp white teeth that glistened with saliva.

The young woman shrieked again, and the young man too, both of them cowering back together against the stone behind them.

The eyes blinked. The mouth closed again. Then it turned away from them and retreated, moving with surprising silence through the forest. The whipping of pine boughs as it went upward—climbing?—was repeated, and then a darker shadow swept over the stars for a moment as the monster flew off into the night.

———•———•———•———

Nicodemus Lewis—who was Nico to his friends, or would be if he had any—stared at the closed, insulated door of his icebox and considered pie for breakfast. He was a big man, six foot three, and still in decent shape, despite a slowly growing set of love handles, which meant it took two slices of pie to make a meal. Ergo, if he had pie for breakfast, he would then be out of pie, since two slices were all that remained.

He briefly opened the door to look, as if the pie might somehow have multiplied in the night, but there were still two slices in the pie tin.

He shut it again before the cold provided by the large block of ice in the upper portion escaped, and considered his conundrum. The pie could be two days' dessert, or one day's breakfast. Which would it be?

His state of deep contemplation was interrupted by a knock on the door, so he sighed, turned away from the icebox, and went to answer it. It was nearly midday, despite being Nico's breakfast time. He tended to keep late hours.

The man standing on his doorstep was short, just a little pudgy, and with far more gray in his hair than Nico's own salt-and-pepper dusting. He was also, unfortunately, very familiar: Bradley Jepson, the mayor of Riverport, and the closest thing Nico had to an employer.

"Nicodemus! Just the man I need to see today!"

"Don't know who else you expected, Mayor Jepson. But come on in."

"Thank you." The mayor took his hat off and hung it on the stand beside the door along with Nico's hat and long coat.

Nico sat down on the threadbare couch in his sitting room, while the mayor took the wingback chair upholstered in faded, balding blue velvet.

"So, to what do I owe the honor?" asked Nico, while in the back of his mind a list of potential problems was scrolling past. He really hoped it wasn't the fish-folk again. He thought they'd all been chased off, if not all killed, but that was always so fraught. Too many people in the town were related to them, merely human enough to not suffer the ocean curse. Killing monsters was one thing; killing somebody's dear old Aunt Evelyn was something else, regardless of how many scales she'd grown or how murderous she'd become.

"There have been several sightings of a creature," said the mayor.

"What kind of creature?" asked Nico, knowing that "creature" covered everything from dear Aunt Evelyn to literal demons from Hell.

"The descriptions differ, and most of the sightings are just footprints—well, not feet, but something—and marks it's left behind. It definitely has wings, three eyes, and some kind of fanged mouth, though. And is black all over. Over ten feet tall, probably, though one account says it was low, like a snake."

"Hmm. Doesn't immediately match anything I know. What was it doing, during these sightings?"

"Nobody knows. It seems skittish, it flies off when people see it."

"I see." That might mean it wasn't dangerous, or that might mean it just wasn't hungry right now, or any number of other things. Nico frowned. "Where are the sightings?"

"They're in the woods, near the edge of town, like it was circling us."

"Interesting. You said it leaves marks. Can you show me some of them?"

"Of course. Now?"

"Eh, I need breakfast first." It *was* going to be pie. There was always a chance he might not be alive for dinner, after all. "I'll join you at the town hall in an hour?"

"Very well. Thank you."

Nico shrugged. "It's what I do." *Until something kills me, at least. Not a lot of monster hunters live to retire . . .* He shrugged off that thought as easily as he'd shrugged off the thanks and rose to escort the mayor out of his house so he could have some pie.

A little over an hour later he was on the town hall's steps, staring up at the stained, faux-Greek facade with its ornate Corinthian columns. Nico himself was more Greek than that thing, even though he'd never set foot in Greece. But his parents had, and his dark, olive-tan skin, curled hair still dark despite the growing gray, and dark brown eyes all showed his origins clearly.

"Nico! I mean, Nicodemus."

Nico grinned. He'd been quite firm with the mayor the last time he'd tried the nickname. It seemed that had made an impression. "Hello, Mayor Jepson."

"Hello. One of the boys is bringing a car around. We'll drive out to see where this creature left its mark."

The car rumbled up a moment later, a dark-skinned man behind the wheel. Nico frowned; "the boys" for grown men had never sat well with him, but now probably wasn't the time to start that argument again.

Nico got in the other front seat, refusing to ride in the back like a spoiled prince, and smiled at the driver, who gave him a smile in return. The mayor, of course, climbed in the back. Then the car was moving, heading down the street with the other cars and the occasional cart or horse-cab, though you saw fewer of those all the time. They made their way past the docks and their fishing fleet—the real heart of the town—and out north, towards the lighthouse. Soon they'd passed the last houses and reached the point where trees closed in all around. Immediately after that the driver pulled the car over to the side of the road, parking in a clear patch where previous tire tracks and footprints showed in the damp soil.

The latter all pointed off into the forest, so Nico didn't have to wait for Mayor Jepson to know what to do; he set off along that track himself, scanning the surrounding woods for signs of anything uncanny. He heard thrashing behind him and chuckled. Mayor Jepson was obviously unaccustomed to moving amid the undergrowth.

They didn't have to go far, else Nico would have left the mayor far behind. He could still see light amid the trees from the open strip of the road when he arrived at what was definitely his destination.

The undergrowth was pressed down and broken across a small clearing where a rotted, fallen tree trunk showed what had happened to open the area to the sky. It looked as if something heavy had trampled it, but where there was bare earth the marks were nothing like footprints, more like the winding paths of snakes. Whatever had left them was no snake, though, for the trees nearby had a series of deep claw marks in the bark, at perhaps fifteen feet up, sap beginning to dribble from the wounds, the trees' blood oozing like honey.

"Interesting." Nico looked around, not stepping into the space yet. He saw footprints over the strange marks, here and there, but he wasn't going to add his own to them; that would only erase what evidence remained. Instead he began to circle, walking around the trees that ringed the clearing, peering at the trampled ground but not touching anything.

"Do you see anything important?" asked the mayor as he blundered up to the clearing.

"Perhaps," said Nico. "And please stop there, don't move."

"Ah . . ." The mayor halted for a moment with one foot in the air, then slowly put it down. "Alright."

"Thank you, sir," said Nico, absently, continuing his circle. Suddenly he halted, and reached out carefully to pick up something that rested amid the roots of one towering pine, well-marked with deep scratches. "Ah."

"What? What is it?"

"Nothing I didn't already know, but potentially useful all the same," said Nico, holding it up.

"Oh. A feather."

"A very interesting feather," replied Nico. Nico knew enough of birds to know that it was a covert feather, one of the smaller feathers that rested above the primary and secondary flight feathers on a bird's wing. It was also nearly as long as his forearm. Few earthly birds had primaries this long; none at all had coverts of such a size. Of course he had already known that the creature was large and flighted, but now he had a concrete connection to it, and there were things that could be done with that.

Nico continued his circle, but beyond being certain that whatever it was had claws, and wings, and didn't have feet but perhaps some kind of serpentine lower half, he determined nothing whatsoever.

"Well?" said the mayor as Nico came back around to where he stood.

"I've learned something, but not much. I'll stay on the job, though. Assuming it is a job?" He gave the mayor a significant look.

"Oh. Yes, it is a job. I'll fill out the paperwork and have the secretary send you a check right away."

"Thank you, sir," said Nico, giving a respectful nod to Mayor Jepson. Not that he had any real respect, but he needed to eat, so . . . "Shall we head back to the car?"

"Right, yes," said the mayor, looking down at his now-scuffed shoes.

They returned to the car and the patient driver returned them to town, even dropping Nico off at his house first rather than going directly to the town hall.

Home again, Nico went to the desk that shared space with bookshelves, the couch, the chair, and everything else in his front room. The house only had three rooms, so one had to be sitting room, office, and workroom all at once. He spread a map of the area out on the desk, then took the feather that he'd carefully cradled all this time—black and glossy with hints of bluish iridescence—and set it atop the map.

Nico straightened, focusing, trying to clear his mind. He picked up the feather, holding it in the middle, setting the tip of the shaft to the map. He started well out into the water, away from everything, then he closed his eyes for a moment, letting his hand relax until he was just barely holding the feather. He was no magician, but dowsing required very little skill and no true power. With something like the feather to use, especially, it should be easy.

Indeed, the feather's tip was dragged almost instantly across the map, going in from the ocean to touch at the head north of town where the lighthouse stood. It circled there once before dipping south, running along the coast until it reached the town, then arcing around it, touching the woods along the borders of it and coming back to the coastline just south of town. Then the feather retraced that route, back to the lighthouse, and north along the coast from there for two or three miles. The feather began to run back down to the lighthouse once more, but Nico gripped it and lifted it from the map. It would repeat its course as long as he let it, but he'd gotten the information he needed.

Not something from the town, nor something from the sea. Not something from the forest, either, but something that moved along the borders between.

Interesting.

The road was barely more than a pair of ruts, as Nico strode down it later that evening. It had obviously once been graded and graveled, but had seen better days. Trees pressed close around it, but it did at least see enough use that none of them intruded on the road proper.

Nico walked briskly along it, looking towards the loom of the head in front of him, where a black basalt massif rose up out of the forest only to plunge again into the sea, the furthest tip of it crowned with the white spire of the Riverport Lighthouse.

He'd gotten a ride along the coast road most of the way here, but the coast road looped inland rather than climbing the cliffs, so the road to the lighthouse broke away half a mile or so short of it.

The road Nico followed almost immediately began climbing, making a series of switchbacks as it ascended the shallower southern, landward side of the head. The northern side was connected to higher hills of basalt, dotted with trees, that the coast road wound between further east. They were part of the ancient lava flow that had created the head, and much of the geography of the area, tens of thousands of years ago.

Trees covered the slope, and as Nico continued he soon noticed a spot like the one the mayor had shown him, where massive claws had marked wood a good fifteen feet up. It wasn't directly on the road, but it was visible from there. Nico took a moment to thread his way through the undergrowth to the spot. He didn't find any feathers, but he got a clearer impression of the creature's bizarre tracks. They definitely reminded him of the marks a snake might leave behind, marks of something long and narrow. A snake the size of those marks would hardly have indented the pine-needle-strewn earth here, though; whatever had left these marks had been quite heavy. Nico frowned, trying to picture it. Something snake-shaped, at least on its lower part, and narrow, no bigger around than Nico's own leg, but at least ten feet tall, winged, and clawed. The image wouldn't come together for him.

Perhaps the lower part wasn't actually snake-like, but dragged on the ground somehow?

None of it matched any creature he knew, so he shrugged and returned to the road, continuing his climb up to the lighthouse.

He came out of the trees and onto the head, where trees had long ago been uprooted to make room for the lighthouse and the attached keeper's cottage. Wind struck him immediately, blowing hard off the ocean, and Nico noticed that the sky was dark with clouds, the day gone cold. He pulled his coat tighter around him and held his hat on. He'd worn the coat as much for its many inner pockets as for its warmth, but now he was glad of the latter too.

The lighthouse rose before him, the light not yet lit. At its base was the keeper's cottage, a tiny thing beside the lighthouse's bulk, but made of the same white-painted stone. A little fenced-off area between the cottage and the wood held a garden, verdant and lush, full of vegetables, herbs, and even flowers.

Nico followed the path that led from a graveled patch where the road stopped, around the garden, and to the cottage door, where he knocked briskly.

It didn't open immediately, but Nico waited, and eventually the door swung inward to reveal the lighthouse keeper.

Nico's first impression was that the keeper was a little mouse of a man. He was short, not quite coming up to Nico's shoulder, and wearing an oversized beige cable-knit turtleneck and khaki slacks. His feet, oddly, were bare. His hair was a washed-out ash blond, straight, fine, and desperately in need of a cut, for it was falling into his eyes, which were pale gray. His skin was pale too, the color of somebody who never saw the sun, and his features were narrow, his chin pointed, nearly girlish. There were lines of tired strain around his eyes, but his face was otherwise youthful. He could have been almost any age, especially since gray would hardly show in the washed-out color of his hair.

"Hello. I'm Nicodemus Lewis." Nico held out his hand.

"Ah." The keeper made an awkward gesture with his right hand, which Nicodemus saw was curled in a claw-like posture, apparently damaged from some past injury. "Sorry. I'm Azrael Slavich."

Nicodemus almost said something about the odd name, but then he could hardly talk, given what his parents had saddled him with. "Good to meet you. If you're not busy right now, can I take a moment of your time?"

"I was about to go light the lantern up top, actually. With the storm coming on it's already dark enough. You can come along if you like, though, or wait down here." He stepped back, gesturing inside.

The cottage was tiny, not just in comparison to the massive lighthouse. There was only a single room, one end holding a bed, the other a small kitchen, a desk and chair set beneath the diamond-paned window in between. The rest of the walls were covered by bookshelves, stuffed full of books, giving way only where the two doors stood—the one Nico now stepped through and the one leading into the lighthouse proper.

Everything was neat and tidy, not merely clean but precise, the books in ruthless order, the papers on the desk neatly squared up and aligned, the bed tidily made up. The closest thing to disorder was a book sitting crookedly atop the desk as if just now discarded, though of course it had a bookmark in it and wasn't laid carelessly facedown the way Nico would have left it.

Azrael shut the door behind him, closing out the cutting wind. Nico hadn't realized quite how bad it had gotten until he was out of it. He pulled his coat and hat off with a sigh.

"Can I take your coat?" asked Azrael, reaching for it.

Nico yanked back the armful of heavy fabric on instinct. "No! Ah. No, I've got it. Thanks." He hung it carefully on one of the coat hooks by the door, beside an oilskin jacket that had to be Azrael's, and tried not to flush at his reaction. Being overprotective of a coat would make people think he'd gone mad.

But Azrael only nodded and crossed the room to the other door. "Do you want to come up with me? There are quite a lot of stairs, so you don't have to."

"I've never seen a lighthouse from the top. I'll come, sure."

The interior of the lighthouse was a space not much larger than the cottage; the wall the door pierced was something like a yard thick. There were more bookshelves against the walls in here, Nico saw with amusement, as well as a tidy stack of crates, boxes, and barrels tucked against the wall space not occupied by shelves or stairs.

Those were a metal spiral, going upwards in a way that was nearly dizzying when Nico peered up through the center. A pair of jerry cans sat beside the stairs, and Azrael picked up one of them, lifting it so easily that for a moment Nico thought it must be empty. Yet it seemed the short man was actually quite strong, for it swung from his left hand very much as if it were full. He started up the stairs, and Nico followed, his booted feet making the metal ring.

They climbed.

Then they climbed some more.

And then they kept climbing.

There were no progress marks, no distinct flights, just the endless around and around and around. Nico tried to estimate how tall the lighthouse was. A hundred feet?

Nico's thighs began burning, and he found himself slowing, breathing hard as he fell behind Azrael, who climbed on effortlessly, despite the weight of the can he carried.

"How . . . how high is this thing?" Nico called out, pausing to catch his breath.

Azrael paused too, now a quarter-turn above him on the spiral, and looked back. "Sixty-eight feet," he said.

"Damn. It feels like a mile tall, at least," said Nico.

Azrael smiled, a tiny curve of narrow lips, and said, "You don't have to finish. I remember how hard the climb was when I started."

"No, I still want to see the view," said Nico stubbornly, aware that it was at least half pride that made him want to keep going. He was supposed to be a strong, fit, tough guy. Illogical as it was, knowing that Azrael must do this climb at least twice a day, Nico couldn't let himself be shown up by the mousy little man. At least not any more than necessary. "You go on, I'll catch up."

"Alright."

Nico waited a moment longer, listening to the quiet, Azrael's still-bare feet making no noise at all as he climbed, the only sound the muffled whine of the wind outside the thick walls and Nico's own rapid breathing. Then he started climbing again.

He had to pause once more, but finally he reached the top, where glass walls encircled the massive lamp of the lighthouse's namesake light.

Azrael was filling a reservoir with clear fluid from the jerry can, sending the sharp scent of kerosene into the air. The reservoir was beneath the cylindrical mesh "wick" of the lamp, like an ordinary kerosene lamp but on a massive scale. A vast, rippled disk of glass stood on the seaward side of the light, to focus it outward, and Nico found his gaze drawn past it, out to the sea, where the sun was showing beneath the clouds, sending golden beams upward as it sank to touch the water. The sky above was nearly black now, and the howl of the wind loud as it whined and wailed around the lighthouse.

"There." Azrael set the now-empty can aside and pulled out a lighter. That seemed strangely prosaic, but the little flame he flicked to life there lit the huge lamp readily, light springing up as the wick became a pillar of brilliant fire.

"That's one big candle," said Nico. There was something compelling about the huge flame, though it was too bright to comfortably stare at.

Azrael chuckled, a warm, deep sound of amusement. "That it is. Now, time to go back down."

Nico groaned. "God."

"Unless you want to live up here, I'm afraid needs must."

Nico laughed. "Yeah. Okay, at least down will use different muscles."

"Indeed. Although on the subject of living here, I notice you didn't have a car. If you walked here clear from Riverport, I'd advise against going back tonight. There's quite a storm brewing. You see what it's like out there, and the worst of it hasn't remotely hit yet. You can stay here overnight and go back in the morning."

Nico blinked. He hadn't even thought about his return trip, though he should have. The bizarre monster had been so fascinating, he'd fixated on finding it. Now, though, reality intruded. "Ah . . . thank you. I don't want to impose."

Azrael just shrugged. "Come on, let's go down, and you can tell me what brought you here in the first place."

By the time he reached the bottom, Nico's legs felt like jelly. He was more than grateful to flop down in the chair Azrael offered him. It was built to the smaller man's scale, though, so he had to stretch his legs out or leave his knees comically folded up. Azrael seemed content to perch on the foot of the bed beside him.

"So, ah, what did you need?" he cocked his head to the side, looking like some kind of bird, his pale eyes bright with curiosity.

"Do you know about the monster sightings around town?"

Azrael drew in a sharp breath. "Monster sightings? I . . . no. What kind of monster? Has it hurt anyone? Is it just around Riverport?"

"So far it hasn't hurt anyone, no. In fact it's fled from all encounters I know of, so it might be harmless. But it's definitely capable of harm, given that it seems to like to mark up trees with some kind of claws. The sightings have been around town, but I saw some of the marks on the road up here, near the lighthouse. You probably don't need to fear, though."

Azrael blew out a breath, deliberately lowering his shoulders, which had crept up around his ears. "Yes, I . . . I mean, I'm not a coward! But I'm alone here. A, ah, dangerous monster here sounds quite worrying. Are you, or, uhm, is there an effort to deal with it?"

"As of now, you're looking at the effort." Nico gestured at himself with a wry smile. "And all I'm doing is gathering information. If it proves to be dangerous, though, it will be taken care of. I've taken care of such things before."

Azrael blinked, wide-eyed, again looking bird-like. "Oh! I think I've heard of you, then. When I first started working here everyone was buzzing about it. There was a were-seal, and a monster-killer who'd dispatched it."

"Yeah, that was me." Nico remembered that one very well indeed. Though if Azrael had been working here when that had happened, over fifteen years ago . . . Nico mentally revised his estimate of Azrael's age upward. He had to be in his mid-thirties at least, maybe even as old as Nico himself, who'd passed forty not long ago. Nico also crossed the slight chance that Azrael had something to do with this current monster off of his mental list. If he'd been here that long, it would be a stretch to connect him to a newly arrived creature just because it had visited an obvious landmark like the lighthouse. "She was dragging people out of boats and eating them. A lot of were-folk can co-exist with humans, but not if they're doing that sort of thing."

Azrael nodded. "Yes, I can understand that. I, uhm, hope this new monster is a kind that can co-exist? If it's wandering up near me, well, you understand, I'm sure."

"I do, yes." Nico nodded. "Have you seen anything unusual lately? It seems to be winged, so odd birds in the distance, shadows where there shouldn't be, noises, strange tracks, anything like that?"

Azrael shook his head. "I'm afraid not. I spend most of my time indoors, reading. I only go out to do my morning gardening once I've put out the light for the day, before going to bed. I haven't seen anything unusual during that, though."

"Perhaps from the top of the lighthouse? You have such a view here!"

"I do. Sometimes I watch the sunset or the sunrise from up there. But no, I haven't seen anything odd or unusual at all. Admittedly if it's in the forest I wouldn't have, I'm nearly always looking to the seaward side. The ocean is beautiful." He smiled—a soft, wistful expression— before his face returned to what seemed a habitual expression of weary calm.

"Ah well. Let me know if you do? The creature's trail, such as it is, does seem to lead here as much as anywhere."

"How so, if the sightings are mostly around the town?" asked Azrael curiously.

"You get sightings where you have people to sight things," said Nico, grinning. "Most things we humans call 'monsters' stay well away from humanity, and nobody sees them. It's part of why all this activity worries me. A monster who's coming out in the open, well . . . something has gone wrong when that happens, one way or another."

"I see." Azrael nodded solemnly. "I'm afraid they haven't repaired the telegraph line since the last storm that took it down, though, and I hardly ever go into town. I could send a message back with the nice fellow who delivers my supplies, perhaps?"

"Sure. Or I'll check in again. If I'm tracking this thing up and down the coast, I'll probably pass by here now and again. It's a nice place, and you've been a good host."

Azrael blinked at him, his pale cheeks turning pink. "Oh dear! No, I haven't been. Why I haven't even offered you anything to drink! I usually have tea, I could make you some? And I've already had my breakfast, but I'm sure I could get something together for your dinner, if you haven't eaten yet?"

Nico, who'd had either a very late lunch or a very early dinner, was definitely hungry, so he nodded. "I don't need anything much. Some bread and butter or whatever you have that's easy. Tea would be good too. Thanks."

"You're very welcome," said Azrael, rising. He bustled about the kitchen, heating water on top of the old-fashioned wood-fired stove and measuring out tea into two strainers. He didn't have an icebox, Nico noticed, but he vanished into the lighthouse, which was colder than the little cottage, certainly, and came back with a cheese, which he proceeded to cut slices from to put on a plate with crackers that emerged from a cupboard. He did all that with comfortable ease, despite only having full use of one hand.

The kettle whistled, and moments later Nico was presented with a platter of cheese, crackers, and sausage, and a cup of fragrant tea smelling faintly of oranges.

"The tea is bergamot, which I hope you like, that's my favorite. I might have some plain black tea somewhere, but I'm not sure," said Azrael, perching on the bed again with his own cup.

"This is fine, thank you." Nico set the plate on the desk and nibbled the cheese, which turned out to be a sharp, crumbly cheddar. Everything else was good too, and for a while there was silence as he ate and Azrael slowly sipped. The wind was howling outside, and the lighthouse's light showed just enough outside the thick windowpanes for Nico to see that it was raining, heavy drops falling almost sideways, torn by the wind. Inside that was all muffled and distant, though, the cottage pleasantly warm, the food pleasantly good, everything cozy and comfortable.

Azrael sighed contentedly when he'd finished his cup. "When I was young I never had anything like this," he said.

Nico blinked at him. No tea? "Were you poor, then?"

Azrael shook his head, a tiny smile quirking up the corner of his mouth in amusement. "Oh, no. I could have had such things if my kinfolk had valued them. But they were of the opinion that food was for survival, not for pleasure. They also believed that books were solely for necessary education, that games were ridiculous and only for very young children, and a great many more such boring, repressive things."

"Oh. That sounds pretty awful."

"Yes. I was very happy to come here and get this job, well away from all of them." Azrael looked into his empty cup for a while, his expression turning dark. Then he shrugged and rose, carrying the cup to the sink. "I have tea now, and whatever else I like, within reason, so I am well content."

"You don't get lonely out here by yourself?" asked Nico.

Azrael shrugged again. "Oh, from time to time a little company would be nice, but I've always been a solitary sort, and I have my books." He patted the nearest bookshelf, which could be done without moving from almost any point in the cottage.

Nico smiled. "Yeah, I can tell you like to read." He polished off the last of the plate, and sipped a little of the still-warm tea.

"If you're tired, you're more than welcome to take the bed. I'll be up all night, just to be sure the light doesn't go out, so I don't need it."

"Thanks. I keep late hours myself, though, so I'm not tired yet." He glanced down at the desk, at the book there. It had a plain black leather cover with no title on the front. "What are you reading?"

Azrael walked over and plucked it up, turning the spine towards Nico. "A little classical fiction," he said.

Metamorphoses, by Ovid, Volume IV, read the spine. "Huh. I've heard of it, but I've never read it. Long story, then, if there's four books?"

Azrael chuckled. "There are fifteen books, but it's not one story. It's a series of stories, with common themes. Quite ambitious! This volume is the one about lovers."

"Oh! Is it salacious, then?" Nico winked, unable to help the half-flirtation.

"Quite definitely. Although I'm not sure how romantic it is. There's a great deal more rape and tragedy and so on than one would get in a modern romance."

"Ah. I'll pass, then. I like enthusiastic lovers, not reluctant ones."

Azrael nodded. "It's interesting for its place in history, and enjoyable as fiction, but not something I'd want to imitate, no." His cheeks flushed and he added, "Not that I know what I *would* want to imitate. Trying to learn about sex from books is a terrible idea, I suspect."

Nico blinked at Azrael, his own cheeks coloring. "No, one usually learns from experience."

"Sorry, I should change the topic. I don't always remember what I should and shouldn't say to other people." Azrael was still blushing, and he looked away from Nico.

"Hey, no, it's fine. I mean, it's not a topic for a society tea party or anything, but I don't mind. I'm hardly a blushing virgin." He gave Azrael another wink.

Azrael nearly choked on nothing. "I, ah, oh dear."

Nico blinked. "What, you've never?"

"Well . . . no," confessed Azrael. "My options back home were . . . distasteful, let's say, and since then I've been rather isolated out here."

"Oh. Damn. That makes me want to drag you into town and find you a nice lady who can show you how it's done." Nico shook his head. "Though now I'm the one being inappropriate. And I'm not even drunk!" He grinned. He felt strangely fond of the odd lighthouse keeper already. The same sort of mother-hen instincts that had gotten him into killing monsters for a living, probably. He couldn't leave somebody who seemed helpless alone, whether it was physical danger or lack of sex life that was the problem.

With nearly his whole face crimson by now, Azrael shook his head. "You don't need to do that. I'm fine, really."

"Sorry, sorry, I'll leave you be. There's no shame in not having sex, whatever some people might think."

That got another of those little smiles. They were quite endearing, really. "I'm glad you think so. But perhaps we could find something else to discuss, if you want to talk. Or you could borrow a book to keep yourself occupied?"

"Sure, that sounds good. What do you recommend?"

After a lot of narrowing down Azrael's many and enthusiastic recommendations, Nico ended up on the bed with a detective novel, while Azrael sat in his chair with his feet tucked up under him and read his volume of Ovid. The storm continued to rage outside, yet inside Nico felt surprisingly comfortable. Azrael was good company, he decided. Nico didn't find good company often. He didn't get along with most people, so despite living in town, he was in some ways nearly as isolated as Azrael was. It was nice to spend time around somebody without feeling judged, and without feeling the need to impress, behave, or conform to the expectations of "polite" society.

They read together in companionable silence for several hours. Nico eventually began to yawn, though, before his usual post-midnight bedtime, even. But then he'd had an eventful day, so why not rest?

Azrael politely blew out all of the lights, save a single small lantern, using the same kerosene as the lighthouse, but turned down so low it was a faint golden glow, and continued his reading while Nico settled himself beneath the blankets.

He closed his eyes, concentrating on relaxing, on breathing deep and slow. Breathing in, he smelled a hint of warm scent, and nearly chuckled at it. Azrael's scent, of course, since this was his bed, and he would hardly make it up with clean sheets every day, given how difficult washing must be up here. It was unusual, a floral musk with a dusty note that reminded him of feathers, and of books—of course books—but it was entirely pleasant, and he drifted off to sleep surrounded by it.

————•———•———•————

Nico woke with a vague awareness that he'd been dreaming—something about flying, about facing down a dark thing that wanted to steal his wings—but he couldn't recall the details. It hadn't been a nightmare, somehow he'd been spared having his wings ripped off. Someone or something had come to his rescue? The more he tried to remember, the more it slipped away. He opened his eyes and saw morning light coming in through the front window by the door, which faced east. There was no sign of Azrael anywhere.

He stretched, groaning at how sore every muscle in his legs was, but eventually managed to rise. Once upright he went to the kitchen area, where the stove, sink, and cupboards were tucked into the limited space, and found the stove already stoked and warm. It no doubt heated the space as much as cooked. He filled a kettle and put it on, then rummaged in the cupboard for the tea. Just as he was measuring it out Azrael came in through the lighthouse door. "Good morning."

"Morning," said Nico. "I'm making tea, sorry for taking over. I can make you some too?"

"That would be lovely, thank you."

Nico smiled and measured out a second portion of tea leaves, then sat back to wait for the kettle to boil.

Once it whistled he poured the hot water over the tea leaves, savoring the immediate scent of tea and oranges that floated into the air.

Azrael dropped down to sit on the bed, watching Nico as he poured the cups, steam rising from them. Eventually they were ready, and Nico handed Azrael his cup.

"Thank you." The strange man closed his eyes, inhaling the steam over the cup. Nico couldn't help but smile at the shameless hedonism of it.

"Since the storm has blown over, I should probably be going," said Nico.

"Oh. Right." Azrael looked up at him, brows drawn together in a troubled expression. "I have enjoyed having you here more than I expected. I suppose I do like company now and again. So, well, don't hesitate to come back if you need to."

Nico found himself smiling at Azrael's awkward sincerity. "Of course. Just keep your eye out for any sign of this monster."

"I will." Azrael smiled that tiny little half-smile again. Nico found himself thinking it made Azrael look lovely. Something about that little amused lip-quirk transformed him from soberly mousy to sweetly handsome.

Nico and Azrael finished their tea in silence. Then Nico put his cup in the sink, picked up his coat and hat, and headed out the door. Azrael came behind him, still barefoot, but halted at the garden. "Have a pleasant trip back to town," he said.

"Thank you. See you again, I'm sure." Nico waved, and despite having learned nothing of any real use about the monster, he found himself feeling pleased—self-satisfied, even—about the entire affair.

◆　●　●

He walked back down to the coast road, and managed to catch a ride into town not long after he started walking along the edge of the tarmac there. Once back home, Nico sat down in his front room to consider his next course of action. The map was still spread out on his desk, the feather beside it. He took a moment to dowse again, but got the same result. The monster hadn't broadened its territory any further last night, it seemed.

Eventually Nico went out and made his own half-circle around the town's boundaries. In addition to the half-dozen spots where the creature had been seen, he found twice as many places where it had clawed up the trees.

He wondered why it was doing that. Was it like a cat sharpening its claws? Was it marking its territory? Some animals did that, he thought. Given it was an unearthly being, perhaps the reason was stranger than that. Perhaps it was doing some sort of magical working with the marks. Though they looked like simple claw slashes, not like intelligible letters of any sort, but who knew? The Ogham alphabet was made from simple slashes, after all.

Nico didn't get any feel of magic around any of the sites, but he might not—he wasn't wildly sensitive. Perhaps he should ask somebody who was to come out and have a look. By the time he'd done the full circuit around town, though, it was getting dark, so he headed back home.

His own bed, he decided as he lay there, was inferior to the one that Azrael had. He shifted, rolled over, punched his pillow to fluff it up, but couldn't quite find a position that seemed comfortable. Maybe he needed to rub out a quick one. That always did help him sleep, though it always felt sad and pathetic compared to having a lover in his bed.

Now there was a thought: better than him in Azrael's comfortable bed, Azrael in his, here with him. Cuddling a little, perhaps, or perhaps doing more than that.

Nico snorted at himself as he lay there in the dark. It had been *much* too long since he'd had a lover, hadn't it? The last one had been that lovely woman on the other side of the street. She'd been older than him, with a magnificent figure, and her habit of wanting to cuddle after while she chattered on about her children's lives had been sweet.

Then her oldest daughter had finally had a child of her own, and the woman had moved away to be near her grandchild.

The last time he'd had a male lover . . . how long had it been? It was hard to recall. Had that been the younger man he'd met at the bar and had drunken sex with, and then sober sex again on half a dozen different occasions before the fellow had declared it had all been a drunken mistake? Probably. Damn. That had been five or six years ago. Surely Azrael wouldn't do that sort of nonsense, at least? Not that he was likely to be into men himself.

Still . . . Nico thought of that sweet smile. Thought too of how easily Azrael had lifted the kerosene can and how often he climbed the lighthouse stairs, and speculated on the muscles that had to lie under that oversized sweater's loose drape.

It was all too easy to imagine a small, fit, pale-skinned form beneath him, not a mouse at all, but an utterly gorgeous man, moaning and writhing in pleasure as Nico showed him what sex was like.

Fuck.

It had *definitely* been too long, if he was fantasizing about random men he barely even knew.

Still, there was no harm in it, was there? Nico let out a breathy sigh and slipped his hand inside his undershorts. His other hand reached for the nightstand, and the tissues there. Nico closed his eyes, then, curling his hand around his cock. Dammit, this was stupid. But hell. He was already half-hard, he might as well.

He thought about Azrael again. God, it would be so good, he was sure of it. Showing an inexperienced man the give-and-take of sexual pleasure was always good, and there was no way somebody as smart and thoughtful as Azrael would be bad at it. Would he like giving head, Nico wondered? Some men hated it and some men loved it. Nico loved giving it possibly even more than getting it. Sucking Azrael's cock until he went all to pieces with how good it felt . . . God yes, that would be amazing. And the sight of Azrael between his legs, sucking his? That fine, pale hair completely disarrayed, his lips stretched around Nico's cock, his eyes closed in no doubt earnest concentration . . .

Nico groaned, tipping his head back against the pillow, stroking himself steadily. This was so ridiculous! But oh fuck, those images were so, so good. He tensed, breathing faster, more than halfway there already.

He paused a moment to wiggle his undershorts down, then continued, picturing Azrael all sorts of different ways, fantasizing about what he might like, what he might want Nico to do, what Nico might get to do to him.

It took hardly any time at all before he came, seed spurting out into the tissues he'd cupped over his cock, a near-involuntary groan of "Azrael," escaping him.

When it was over he wadded up the tissues and tossed them onto the nightstand to deal with later, then heaved a sigh. "Nicodemus Balthazar Lewis," he said to the empty darkness of his room. "You are a total mess and that was completely pathetic." Masturbating to a pretty man was one thing, but to somebody he'd met rather than a man onscreen at the latest talkie, and one who would probably die of embarrassment if he knew what Nico had done   Well, at least he was absolutely never going to mention it to Azrael, so no harm done, even if he did feel uncomfortable about it.

The bed no longer felt quite so lumpy, though, and his lids were heavy. He closed his eyes again, relaxing, and was asleep almost instantly.

———•———•———•———

Nico stood in yet another stretch of coastal forest, this one north of the lighthouse, not far from a beach where people sometimes vacationed, overlooked by a few beach houses that stood empty most of the year, but were now filling with people as spring warmed towards summer. He looked up at yet another set of claw marks high on the side of a large pine. He'd picked up another feather, too, this one a downy upper covert the size of his palm, unbelievably soft when he stroked it.

He'd hoped that perhaps the end of the line might have some clue about where the monster had come from, or gone for that matter; he didn't know which direction it had moved or if it had done the string of marks in order.

Unfortunately this site was just like all the rest. He'd worn out a lot of boot leather learning nothing much. That was the nature of the business all too often, but knowing that didn't make him happy about it.

He'd reached the end of his ideas, though. There was nothing special about either end of the monster's trail, nor about the center, he'd checked that too. There was nothing in the town, nobody had seen it by the beach houses, and though it definitely had been around the lighthouse, it didn't seem to have left any marks at the place itself. So where did that leave him?

Waiting for it to do something else, he knew, unless Azrael had spotted it.

Well, he had nothing better to do, so why not?

It was dark by the time he reached the lighthouse, and his stomach was rumbling. He'd walked all the way out so he could check every part of the monster's path. He'd gotten a ride part of the way back, but they hadn't been willing to detour up to the lighthouse, so he'd had to walk that last half-mile. The beacon at the top had come on just as he'd begun the trek, and he'd smiled to see it, remembering Azrael lighting it the other night.

It was a good thing, though, that he didn't need to climb all those stairs again tonight, for he was footsore and exhausted as he knocked on the cottage door.

Azrael opened it almost immediately, looking startled. "Nicodemus?"

Nico couldn't help but take a moment to drink in the sight of Azrael. He looked as good as ever, wearing another loose cardigan that cloaked his figure, but made him look soft and appealing, while his sharp-featured face was lovely, untidy hair falling over his forehead, making Nico want to brush it back. He did his best to shake that thought off, pushing back the faint memory of a night spent fantasizing about Azrael's body, and waved his hand in a hopefully careless gesture. "You can call me Nico. But anyway, sorry to bother you, I just wanted to ask if you've seen any sign of the monster around here in the last two days?"

Azrael shook his head. "Everything's been completely ordinary here. Has it been bothering the town?"

"No. As far as I can tell it appeared, marked up a bunch of trees, and left. Asking you was my last chance to learn anything new, so I guess unless it turns up again, it's case closed."

Azrael smiled, no doubt relieved at the thought that the monster wasn't lurking around anymore. "Sorry I couldn't be of more assistance. But you look exhausted, come in and sit down for a while. You can stay the night again if you like too, I won't need the bed until mid-morning."

"That is very kind of you. Thanks." Nico came inside and collapsed onto the bed. "I think I've taken about half my boot soles off over the last few days."

Azrael chuckled. "The benefits of not wearing shoes, I suppose? Though if I had to walk all the way to town, I'd probably wear my own skin off, so maybe not."

"Hah." Nico managed a tired grin. "Why don't you wear shoes?"

"I do if I have to, I own a pair of decent boots. I just don't like them." Azrael shrugged. "I see no reason to wear them if they're not necessary."

"Fair enough." Nico pulled his own boots off slowly, sighing in relief once they were removed.

"Are you hungry? Can I get you anything?" asked Azrael, standing next to the bed and shifting from foot to foot uncertainly.

Nico smiled. "I did miss dinner, so yeah, something would be nice. Don't put yourself out for me, though. A little of that cheese or whatever would be fine."

"I had actually been debating if I felt like cooking myself something or not. But with two to cook for, well, the effort seems worth it. Do you like fish?"

Nico blinked at him. "Yeah, I do. You go out fishing?"

Azrael smiled. "It would take a very long line to fish from here, and be quite a bother to go somewhere more suited. No. I get food delivered every week, though, and that was, well, your this morning, my yesterday before bedtime. So I have a few fresh things, including a fish packed in ice that I must eat either now or for my 'dinner' come morning, before it spoils. So please, allow me."

"That sounds good. Thank you. Can I help with any of it?"

Azrael hesitated, and he bit his lower lip. "Ah. I think you would be in the way? I don't know how much you'll like my cooking, though. I've never cooked for anyone else before. I have cookbooks, of course, but . . ."

Nico nodded and settled himself back on the bed—once again neatly and tidily made, he noticed—and watched Azrael bustle about the kitchen. He was wearing a different bulky sweater today, in a baby blue that brought a hint of color to his gray eyes. He poked up the fire with an expert touch, then got out a heavy cast iron pan, which he oiled before setting on the stovetop to heat. Then he vanished into the lighthouse, where presumably the fish was waiting in the cooler space.

Returning with it, he got out a chopping board and knife and neatly trimmed off the head and fins, but not the skin, before rummaging in the cupboard and pulling out various spices. The fish was soon stuffed with things, including what Nico recognized as garlic and dill, and then dropped into the pan, where it sizzled immediately. Azrael put a cover over it and smiled. "There. It will still be a while, it needs to cook on both sides, but hopefully not too much longer. If you don't want to wait, I could get you something meanwhile?"

"Eh, I don't need an appetizer. That's already starting to smell great." The scent of seared fish skin and garlic was beginning to waft through the air.

Azrael smiled, his cheeks dusted with a faint blush. "That's good. I should watch it, though, I don't want to get distracted by you and burn it."

Nico nodded, not sure how to respond to that. Was that . . . a flirtation? Was he saying Nico was distracting in a good way? A bad way? A merely neutral way because anybody might be?

Fortunately Azrael didn't seem to expect any response; he was busy in front of the stove, getting out plates, tending to the fish, just bustling around and keeping busy. Nico flopped back and closed his eyes, feeling every mile he'd walked today. He wasn't tired in a sleepy sense, but he was exhausted all the same.

He stared up at the ceiling, which had exposed beams, he noted, and a sub-layer of plywood beneath the shingles he'd seen from the outside.

There were no cobwebs up there, though. Did Azrael sweep it? With what? It wasn't that high but it was above his reach. Nico smiled at himself and let his mind wander as he waited, the little cottage filling with the scent of fish and herbs.

Eventually Azrael said, "It's done," and carried two plates over. He set them both on the desk, so Nico moved to the end of the bed, next to it. "I didn't debone the fish," added Azrael, "so make sure you get all the little bones out before you swallow."

"Right." Nico nodded and took a bite. It was perfect, firm without being rubbery, savory and spiced just so, and sure he had to pull two fine fish bones out as he chewed, but that was fine.

"How is it?" asked Azrael, his expression hesitant.

"Delicious," said Nico, smiling. He would have inhaled the whole plate, if it weren't for the bones, but even with that slowing him down it didn't take long for him to eat every scrap of it.

Azrael took longer, eating with finicky precision. He made a neat pile of tiny bones on his plate, and when everything was gone he leaned back in his chair. "I enjoyed that. I'm glad you did too!"

"You're a good cook," said Nico. "Better than I am."

"Well, thank you," was Azrael's reply. He picked up the plates and set about cleaning. Nico almost offered to help, but he was tired and contented and couldn't quite bring himself to get up. In any case there wasn't that much to clean, and only room for one at the sink next to the stove.

As Nico sat back on the bed he found himself worrying over the problem of the mysterious monster again.

"Shall I turn off the lights so you can sleep?" asked Azrael, sitting back in his chair.

Nico shook his head. "No. My mind's running like a race car. I wouldn't be able to sleep."

"Oh? What sort of thoughts are keeping you awake?" Azrael tilted his head to the side, birdlike, and blinked at Nico.

"I keep thinking about this monster. I wish I could make better sense of it."

"I see."

"My first thought was that it sharpened its claws like a cat, but if it was doing that, why all along the coast here, why not in one spot? Then I thought it was marking its territory, but if it's doing that, why a line? Shouldn't it be encircling something? And why is there nothing at the center of that line? The nearest thing of note to the middle is the lighthouse, but it doesn't seem to have actually come here, except perhaps passing by overhead." Nico shook his head. "For that matter, why did it circle around the town the way it did? If it wants to avoid the town, why not stay away from it entirely? If it's interested in the town, why not go inside the boundaries? There are trees there, and if it's winged it could easily land in the park or in the street at night. I'd feel better if I understood what was going on."

"Ah." Azrael nodded. "That's a feeling I know very well. But if this monster isn't human, why must he have a motivation that's comprehensible to humans? Perhaps there's nothing to understand."

"True enough. He, though? You think the monster is male?"

Azrael chuckled. "I merely read too many books in English, which treats 'he' as the default much of the time. Your monster is as likely to be without gender, or hermaphroditic. Any number of animals are, you know."

"Hah! Indeed. He's not 'my' monster, though. I'm merely tasked with dealing with him."

"If you do find him, what will you do about him?"

Nico shrugged. "It depends. If he's a thinking being that can be reasoned with, I'll try to reason with him. If he's merely an animal . . . well, I might try to drive him off, but I'll more likely kill him, just to know he's been dealt with. And either way, if he refuses to be reasoned with or driven off, I'll kill him."

Azrael's expression was sober as he nodded. "You are charged with protecting people, so that's understandable. It seems like grim business to kill things, though, even monsters."

"It can be, yes. But someone has to do it."

"I shall wish you luck, then, but the kind of luck where your monster can be reasoned with and you've no need to harm him." Azrael smiled, that amused little half-smile that did odd things to the pit of Nico's stomach. He couldn't help but smile back.

"Odds are nothing at all will happen. There's been no sign of him since the initial sightings. He's probably gone back wherever he came from, never to return. I'll keep checking now and again for anything new along the line of marks, but I don't know if I'll find anything."

Azrael looked thoughtful. "Would you like to stay here, then?"

"Uhm . . ." Nico blinked at him.

"You said the lighthouse seems to be close to the middle of your monster's territory, if that's what he's doing by clawing up trees. Would it be easier to keep your eyes out for him reappearing if you were here, rather than all the way at the far end of things in town?"

"Huh. I . . ." Nico hesitated. It wouldn't be that much easier, especially since it would be hard to get word of new sightings to him up here. And yet . . . He looked at Azrael, who was still smiling faintly. Azrael absently brushed a strand of hair out of his eyes, the warm lamp light touching their pale gray with gold. "Yeah, sure," Nico found himself saying. "Thanks! I'll try to not be too underfoot."

Azrael leaned forward and reached out, setting his hand on Nico's arm. His fingers were cool and callused. "I've found your company very pleasant so far. I even missed you a little bit yesterday. I have my books, but it's nice to have someone here."

Nico felt an electric shiver go through him at the touch. Damn. He was probably getting himself in trouble here.

"I don't know much about these things, but it seems as though you find my company pleasant as well?" Azrael's gaze caught his, his expression serious.

"I, er, yes, very pleasant."

Azrael leaned back, removing his hand, and a warm smile blossomed on his lips. "That's good. I wouldn't want you to be stuck here with someone you disliked."

"No, anything but." Nico felt the electricity slowly subside, but it didn't entirely go away. Azrael was right there, looking equal parts adorable and handsome as he smiled, and Nico was having trouble keeping his thoughts from focusing on that.

Fortunately Nico managed to remember the detective novel he'd started on his last visit, and Azrael retrieved it from where he'd reshelved it, a bookmark now neatly tucked into where Nico had absently set it down on its face. After another couple of chapters Nico had settled enough to feel properly sleepy, and the other night was repeated, Azrael putting out all but one lamp.

Settling down amid bedding that still smelled ever so faintly of Azrael's scent, Nico's last thought as he began to drift was to notice how good Azrael looked, bent over his book, in the soft light of his single, candle-bright lamp.

———•———•———•———

Nico was sitting on the grass, in the shade of the lighthouse, while a pleasant breeze ruffled his hair and occasionally the pages of his book too. Azrael was inside sleeping, so Nico had been left to his own devices, and for now he had decided he might as well take a break.

He heard the sound of an approaching engine and looked up from his book curiously. Mindful of Azrael, he tucked a bookmark properly into it with a smile before rising to see who would be up here. Whatever it was puttered and sputtered and seemed to struggle up the slope. When it came into view it was a small motorbike, the rider nearly invisible behind helmet and goggles.

They pulled up in the graveled patch as Nico walked over, then took off the helmet and goggles, revealing the familiar features of Mayor Jepson's driver.

"Hello there! What brings you chasing after me?" asked Nico, though he was pretty sure he knew the answer.

"Mayor Jepson wants to have a progress report. I am informed it has been 'a week' and you should be earning your paycheck."

Nico snorted. "I still haven't *gotten* said paycheck, and it's been not quite five days. I'll write up a progress report and send it along, though. I can do that now, if you're willing to wait?"

"I'm on the clock," said the man, smiling.

Nico chuckled. "Then I won't rush."

He slipped inside, moving as quietly as he could to avoid disturbing Azrael, who was of course asleep, the curtains drawn over the window, keeping the room in darkness save for a hint of light leaking around them, and now around the door Nico had left cracked open.

It didn't take long to find paper and pencil in the neatly organized desk, and to dash out a report, complete with flowery, formal language, about what he knew so far. He folded it up, found an envelope, and stuffed it inside. Then he slipped back out the door, opening it no more than necessary. "Here you go. He'll probably be disappointed, but I've found all there is to be found for now."

"Got it." The man took the envelope and tucked it inside his jacket. "Anything else I should tell him?"

Nico smiled. "I'm tempted to say that if I don't get my check soon I'll start seeing if I can get a monster or two to rampage through the town . . . but I don't know if I could and I know I shouldn't. He only needs to pay me for the five days, if nothing else comes up, though."

"Gotcha." The man grinned broadly. "By the way," he added, "apparently the mayor is putting some pressure on to get the telegraph line up here repaired."

"Oh? That will be convenient, once it happens. Though I imagine it'll be months."

"Oh, yes. He had many words to say for the stupidity of people who thought that the lighthouse didn't need a line of communication. Why, if he'd been able to telegraph and ask if you were here, he could have saved himself a whole fifteen minutes of his time, and me at least two hours!" The man laughed.

"Hmm. Stupidity, you say? But things like a telegraph line would be in the town budget, that the mayor himself approves."

"He was the one who removed that particular item from it last time, I believe." The man flashed another brilliant grin, then donned his goggles and helmet. With a wave he hopped on his bike and sped off, leaving Nico alone once more, but feeling entirely too cheerful.

He picked his book back up and leaned against the lighthouse wall with a smile on his face. Being unable to solve the riddle of this particular monster was annoying, but seeing the mayor shown up was always amusing, and being up here, away from everything, with the fascinating and attractive Azrael soon to wake . . . Well, he had certainly been in worse places!

$$\bullet \qquad \bullet \qquad \bullet$$

"You know, I should ask, do you have any books on supernatural creatures?" said Nico. He'd finished the detective novel, and didn't feel in the mood to read, exactly, but he did enjoy sharing silence with Azrael, now that he'd woken, and didn't know what else to do with himself. A little studying wouldn't be a bad idea, though, if Azrael had any books he himself didn't on the subject.

Azrael looked up from his own book and smiled, which continued to do things to Nico. "In fact I do. The nonfiction is in the lighthouse. I'll show you."

The bookshelves in the lighthouse were, of course, organized by topic as meticulously as any library, and Azrael went directly to a particular one. "Here. Starting with this," his finger rested on a slim little volume, "and going down to here, all these books deal with non-human beings that are more than animals in some way."

"Thanks." Nico scanned over the spines, recognizing many of them. He pulled out a few to inspect further, but didn't find much that grabbed his attention. Although there was a fascinating copy of an old bestiary whose illustrations tempted him to page through it. "Too bad I don't read Latin."

"I do," noted Azrael. "Else I wouldn't have bought the book. Would you like me to translate it for you?"

"If it's not a lot of trouble?"

Azrael shook his head. "Not at all."

They ended up sitting together on the bed, since Nico wanted to see the illustrations and Azrael needed to see the text in order to translate and read it out.

Nico didn't mind, though the awareness of the fact that Azrael's leg was touching him might make concentrating on the book difficult. The way Azrael had immediately sat down so close and put the book across both their laps suggested he didn't mind either.

As Azrael began reading—slowly, sometimes halting and going back as he attempted to render the Latin accurately—Nico found himself leaning in more and more. He could excuse it as wanting to better see the fascinating and often strange illustrations, but he knew perfectly well that he wanted to feel Azrael's shoulder against his, and have their heads nearly touching. Azrael leaned in just as much, though.

The bestiary wasn't one of the little ones aimed at children, full of moral lessons, but it wasn't that long, either. It was still at least an hour short of sunset when Azrael reached the end and closed the cover.

He set the book aside, but didn't move away. He didn't even straighten, keeping his shoulder against Nico's. Nico found himself not knowing what to do with his hands, having the urge to put the one that currently rested on his knee on Azrael's knee instead. He looked over at Azrael, who was looking back, cheeks flushed, expression uncertain. Azrael's hand crept over and settled, the touch so light Nico almost couldn't feel it, on Nico's leg. "Uhm. Nico?"

"Yes?"

Azrael swallowed hard and leaned ever so slightly closer. "I, uhm . . . I've mentioned I don't have any experience, but . . ."

Nico couldn't resist a moment longer; he closed the last few inches between them and kissed Azrael. Azrael made a little humming, pleased sound, and all the tension seemed to go out of him at once, his hand resting fully on Nico's leg, his other arm sliding around Nico's waist. He kissed back, awkwardly but eagerly, and when Nico finally pulled back from the kiss, Azrael was breathing fast, eyes wide and shining.

"Oh. That was . . ." He blinked, then shook his head.

"You've never even kissed someone before?" said Nico gently. Azrael shook his head. He lifted his hand—the right one—from Nico's leg, but Nico put his own hand over it and kept it there. The way the fingers wouldn't completely unfold felt odd, but Nico didn't mind it. He began stroking his own fingers over the back of it, and Azrael relaxed again and sighed.

"No, I haven't. I . . . It's hard to explain."

"You don't need to explain if you don't want to."

"It's just that I, well, I was engaged, you see. It was an arranged marriage. My family set it up for me. She was quite enthusiastic about marrying into my family. Not so much about me. I couldn't stand her. So we never, well . . ." He shrugged. "Getting away from her was part of why I ended up out here, in the middle of nowhere." He flicked a little smile at Nico and added, "Though in some ways experience with her wouldn't be terribly relevant to, ah, you. I mean . . . If you . . . Oh dear. Forgive me, I really don't know what I'm doing at all, though."

"I'll be happy to show you," said Nico, and he kissed Azrael again, deeply this time, his tongue pressing between Azrael's lips. With a tiny, startled inhalation, Azrael parted them. He tasted faintly of the same floral note that scented his bed, bitter and sweet at once. Nico had never experienced anything quite like it.

Azrael turned more fully towards Nico, putting both arms around him. When Nico broke off this kiss Azrael hesitated only a moment, flushed and panting, before climbing onto Nico's lap and kissing him, this time his own tongue asking entrance, slipping between Nico's parted lips to explore him. He was apparently a fast learner, his awkwardness dropping away rapidly. He kissed hard, tongue delving deep, and he pressed his body to Nico's, fervently eager. Perhaps it was no wonder after having been alone and untouched for so long. Perhaps it had nothing to do with Nico himself. It was still both flattering and arousing, and Nico responded, sliding his arms around Azrael in turn, letting them wander up and down his back. He soon slipped them beneath the loose cardigan Azrael was wearing, and beneath his shirt too, feeling the warmth of his skin and the hardness of his muscles.

Azrael made a soft, needy sound into the kiss, his left hand fisting in Nico's shirt. He pulled back a moment later, once again panting fast, but then drew in a deep breath and blew it out in a heavy sigh. His eyes flicked to the window, where the angle of the light made it clear the sun was nearly to the horizon. "Unfortunately I have to go light the lantern. And after that I should probably cook something."

Nico nodded. "I'm not going anywhere, I'll be here when that's done."

Azrael smiled and gave Nico one more kiss, swift and sweet, then climbed out of his lap. "That's . . . good. I'll be back."

Nico waited, patiently enough, paging through the bestiary again and trying to remember everything Azrael had said about the pictures. It wasn't long before Azrael reappeared, a little brown glass jug in his hand.

"What's that?" asked Nico.

"Maple syrup. The real stuff." Azrael smiled. "I'm going to make flapjacks. Do you want some?"

"Absolutely. Can I help?"

"It's a small kitchen. You can find another book while you wait?" Azrael began getting things together. Nico went out into the lighthouse to look over the section on monsters again, and found something he'd only read once and didn't own, so he pulled out the book on demons and settled back into the bed, more comfortable than the too-small chair, to read while Azrael cooked.

It all felt wonderfully comfortable and cozy, in a way Nico had never experienced before. He could dimly recall, from his earliest childhood, before his parents had been killed, that life had been like this, with his mother cooking and his father reading out loud to her from the newspaper.

Nico barely saw the words on the page, he simply leaned back against the wall, legs spread across the bed, book in his lap, and relaxed. This was so perfect.

The flapjacks were good, fluffy and drenched in syrup. Nico ate his fill, and insisted on doing the washing up this time. Azrael let him, settling onto the bed with a book while he did.

When he was done, Nico hesitated a moment between the bed and the chair. He probably should just sit on the chair and read himself, but the bed was more comfortable. And perhaps Azrael might like another kiss or two. But perhaps he didn't, and Nico would hardly want to be too pushy.

Azrael solved the dilemma by scooting over where he sat on the bed and patting the spot beside him. Nico immediately settled himself there, close enough that their legs were touching. Azrael set aside his book, bookmark tucked neatly into it, and rested his hand on Nico's leg. He began stroking his fingers gently up and down. "It's funny . . . I didn't know how much I wanted to be touched before now. I suppose you can't miss what you've never had."

"I'd be happy to touch you as much as you like," said Nico, smiling, a flicker of arousal re-awakening in his core. He turned towards Azrael, pulling him in close. Azrael smiled and climbed back into Nico's lap, which still put his head a little lower, since he was so short and Nico so tall, but he slid his hand around the back of Nico's head and pulled him in, closing that small distance to kiss him.

Nico couldn't resist picking up where he'd left off, but thinking about how Azrael had wanted touch, Nico this time began undoing the cardigan's buttons rather than sliding his hands under it. Azrael broke from the kiss and shed it willingly, then after just a moment's hesitation he removed his shirt as well.

Nico's eyes roamed over him, taking in his fair, fair skin, obviously never sun-touched, and his broad shoulders and narrow waist, all corded with lean muscle, every bit as good as Nico had imagined. He also took in something he couldn't have imagined: the way the scars that pulled and curled Azrael's fingers ran from his palm up his wrist and then around and up, wrapping his entire arm and spilling out onto his chest and shoulder. They were branched and crooked like lightning, showing shiny and taut against the softer skin around them.

"Can I ask?" Nico said, running his hand down Azrael's arm.

"Don't be outside at the top of a lighthouse when a storm is blowing up."

"Ah."

"It struck the rail, not me, but I was grabbing it, and for whatever reason nobody had put a lightning ground on the railing. There is one now."

Nico gave in to the urge to bend and kiss the end of one of the jagged lines that ran out onto Azrael's chest. Azrael drew in a sharp breath, then let it out in a long sigh. "Oh . . ."

With a smile Nico tipped Azrael out of his lap and onto his back on the bed. He put another kiss over a scar, then began scattering kisses and touches all across Azrael's skin. Azrael reached up to him, touching his body too, so Nico sat back for a moment and stripped off his own shirt before resuming what he'd been doing. Azrael drew both hands down Nico's back, their touches different, one palm flat and the other unable to flatten out, but both warm and welcome.

Nico kissed Azrael again, thrilling when Azrael nearly lunged up to meet him. He was so obviously eager, it was both flattering and arousing. Nico pressed him down, kissing him hard and deep. Azrael moaned into it, squirming under Nico. That made it entirely obvious that Azrael was getting aroused by this, and Nico was sure his own reaction was evident too, the way he was straddling Azrael. He had meant to take it slow in the beginning, to go no further than another kiss or two, but now he couldn't help but want more.

Breaking from the kiss, Nico moved to nuzzle back to Azrael's ear, and nip gently there. Azrael gasped and let out a soft "Oh!" of surprise, which slid down into a moan as Azrael continued. He bit and sucked gently at Azrael's earlobe, drinking in the sounds the smaller man made.

From there Nico couldn't resist nipping down the side of Azrael's neck, which got another gasp, and a shudder, Azrael arching under him for a moment as Nico dared to bite just a little bit harder. "Is that okay?" he murmured.

"God, yes," said Azrael breathlessly.

"Good," said Nico and bit again, harder still.

"Ah!" Azrael grabbed Nico's shoulders, digging the nails of his left hand in. He was arched beneath Nico, pressing their hips tight together. Nico ground down on Azrael, enjoying the feel of the hardness of Azrael's cock against his belly, even through the fabric that still separated them.

That drew Nico's attention, so his next nip was a little lower, and then lower still, until he was leaving a slow trail of nips and kisses down Azrael's chest, then down his belly, only stopping at the waistband of his pants. Nico looked up at Azrael, who was panting hard, hands still on Nico's shoulders. Nico put his own hand on the button that fastened Azrael's pants and said, "May I?"

Azrael lifted his head, looking down, eyes wide and cheeks flushed. "Yes. You . . . Yes, please."

Nico undid Azrael's pants and pulled them down, with Azrael's willing cooperation. He wore knee-length white undershorts beneath, tented up with his erection and damp where he'd already begun leaking pre. Nico planted a kiss at the waistband of Azrael's undershorts, then nuzzled down the length of his cock. Azrael let out an incoherent cry, his fingers digging into Nico's shoulders.

Nico moved back up, pressing his lips to the head of Azrael's cock through the thin fabric, hearing Azrael gasp and moan again. Then he undid the drawstring that held them up and pulled the undershorts down, Azrael eagerly lifting his hips to help and kicking the garment off once it was down low enough.

Surveying his nude body, Nico could hardly believe what he was seeing. Azrael was gorgeous, every line of him strongly muscular, his thighs thick, his abdomen chiseled, like a vision of a strongman, yet short and compact, so much smaller than Nico that he could still manhandle Azrael easily. His pale gray eyes were wide, fixed on Nico, and his chest—as perfectly muscular as the rest of him—was heaving as he trembled with desire.

"Do you want me to go on?" said Nico softly, not wanting to push, wanting to be completely certain Azrael was willing.

"Yes, god, yes," said Azrael.

With a breathless moan Nico ducked his head, drawing his tongue up the length of Azrael's cock. He hadn't done this, hadn't tasted the wonderful muskiness of a man, in so very long. Azrael tasted of musk, yes, and also of that odd floral note, uniquely his own. It made Nico moan again as he lapped at it. It was so different, but so good. Azrael moaned too, his eyes closed, his head tipped back, his hands now gripping the blankets beneath him.

Nico licked up to the head of Azrael's cock, then took it into his mouth, intent on giving Azrael the best first experience he could. It seemed, though, that Azrael was already so worked up that this would take little effort, for with a shocked cry of bliss he came, his seed—thick, bitter floral and salt—spurting into Nico's mouth.

He hadn't been expecting it so soon, so Nico made a muffled sound of surprise, but he managed to keep his lips sealed around Azrael's cock, taking it all in, staying still as Azrael shuddered and twitched beneath him.

When the last few drops were done Nico pulled slowly back and swallowed. "Ah . . . yeah . . ." His mind was hazed with the pleasure of having pleased a partner, something he loved even more than finding his own pleasure.

Nico sat up and climbed off of Azrael, who was lying sprawled on the bed, his eyes half-lidded, unfocused. With a warm smile Nico lay down beside him, resting his hand over Azrael's chest.

They lay together in silence for a long time. Azrael's breath slowed, his body relaxed, but he didn't immediately do or say anything. Nico waited, not minding lying beside him, letting him process what had happened at his own pace. After a long time Azrael said, "I see why people are so obsessed with sexual things."

Nico chuckled. "It's pretty nice, isn't it?"

"Yeah. Thank you."

"Hey, I enjoyed it too," said Nico, snuggling a little closer. Azrael turned to him, wrapping his arms around Nico, nuzzling into his chest. Nico pressed his chin to the top of Azrael's head, enjoying holding the smaller man.

Eventually Azrael pried himself out of Nico's arms and dressed again, while Nico pulled a blanket over himself and drowsed. He thought, as he drifted off, that he was glad the monster's trail had led here. Azrael was odd, but tonight had been very good, and Azrael was as pleasant a companion as Nico had ever known. Perhaps, even if his work didn't keep leading him to the lighthouse, Nico might keep returning anyway.

———•———•———•———

Nico woke from a deep, contented sleep with a start, Azrael's hand on his shoulder.

"What is it?" he said, a lifetime of instinct shocking him instantly to full wakefulness.

"Nothing urgent, I don't think, but there's a message here for you," said Azrael.

"Oh." Nico stretched and rose. He dressed swiftly and strode out of the lighthouse, Azrael following behind him. As Nico had half-expected he saw the little motorbike parked in the gravel lot and the young man who ran Major Jepson's errands standing beside it. The sun was well up, but still short of noon, and Nico couldn't help but yawn again. As he walked past the garden to the gravel lot he found himself wondering what else could possibly be so urgent so soon. There was no way Mayor Jepson would go to any effort to deliver his payment, so it couldn't be that.

That meant it was likely to be bad news.

The man called out cheerfully, "Hey there!" as Nico approached. Not that bad of news, then. Nobody could be dead, with such cheer as that.

"Hello," called Nico in response. "What news?"

"Your monster is back, probably," said the young man, getting Nico's full attention instantly.

"Tell me."

"There were two sightings last night. The three eyes and the big, scary creature were the same. Both said it was reddish, though, not black. The mayor had me drive out and look at the marks you saw last time, and there were new ones, but blackened and burned, over the old ones."

Nico frowned. New behavior? Or worse, a second monster?

"Right. I need to go see. Ah . . ." He looked at the small motorbike. "Can you carry me?"

The man laughed. "Sure, but we'll go half speed."

"Beats walking," said Nico.

Azrael, still at his heels, grabbed Nico's elbow. "Nico . . ."

Nico turned, looking down at Azrael. The lighthouse keeper's brows were knit, his expression fearful.

"Hey, dealing with monsters is what I do. This one's just left his mark and gone, it should be safe," he said.

"I . . . I hope so." Azrael pulled Nico in suddenly and gave him a deep, fervent kiss. Nico made a muffled sound of surprise, then kissed back willingly. "Be careful," said Azrael when he let Nico go.

"I will," Nico promised. He gave Azrael a quick return peck of his own, then turned and climbed up behind the mayor's messenger on his bike, tucking his long legs up awkwardly.

"You know, I never got your name," he said as he settled into place. He thought it would be best not to mention what had just transpired between him and Azrael, and the other man seemed to agree.

"Emmanuel," said the man, grinning. "People call me Manny, if you can't manage the whole of it."

Nico chuckled. "I can manage it, so I'll use whichever you prefer. I'm Nicodemus, but Nico is fine."

"Well, Emmanuel is what my mother named me, so that's who I am," the man said.

Nico smiled and nodded as the motor's hum rose and they started on their way. "Emmanuel it is, then." He gave Azrael a wave, and then the bike was in among the trees and the lighthouse keeper was gone from view, though the top of the lighthouse remained visible behind them all the way. Nico didn't look back, though. Much as he liked Azrael, he had a job to do now, and he needed to focus his full attention on it.

Emmanuel took him to the same spot where he'd found the first feather, just barely outside of town. Nico was pleased to see that this time nobody had been walking over it, and since there'd been a storm since the last time, the new prints were clear in the few open patches of dirt on the forest floor. They were very like what he'd seen before, tracks like a snake's. He could see the gouges he'd seen last time, now crusted over with sap that leaked down the trunk in thick streams. Atop them, though, were fresh marks, the same shape and size, but blackened as if whatever had made them had been red-hot.

"Hmm." Nico circled the area, looking for some additional sign, but found nothing else. No feathers, no other hints at what had happened.

He returned to the road, and Emmanuel drove him into town.

Back home, Nico checked on his mail, which was empty, and his icebox—also empty, even of ice—then shrugged and left again. A swing past the market got him a quick lunch, after which he headed for the town hall to bully his paycheck out of Mayor Jepson. It was his secretary who filled it out, of course, but the mayor was there, hovering. Nico wondered what exactly he did most of the day.

"So, what's out at the lighthouse, that you're staying out there and not in town?" asked the mayor while Nico waited for the check to be done.

"The monster's marks go up a couple more miles north, so the lighthouse is near the middle of it. I figured that's a good place to be, and the keeper has been very accommodating."

"That weirdo? You don't mind him? I almost didn't hire him, wasn't sure a cripple like that could do the job—you know, he's got that weird hand—but it's hard to find people to live in the middle of nowhere and I wasn't going to raise the pay any."

Nico bristled at the way the mayor talked about Azrael, but he was also taken aback. This meant Azrael had gotten his scars before moving into the lighthouse. Had he worked at another lighthouse before? He'd certainly never mentioned anything about that. Had he lied about the scars, then? Or had he intentionally omitted some key details about his background?

"Here you are, Mr. Lewis, sir," said the secretary, interrupting Nico's thoughts by handing over the check.

"Thank you," he said, but as he left he found the question of whether Azrael had lied—and if so, why—lingering in his mind. It probably was only that the real story was somehow uncomfortable to tell. Yet it was hard for Nico to dismiss it. If Azrael had lied about his hand, what else might he be hiding?

———•———•———•———

Nico lucked out, catching a ride out of town, and was once more dropped at the road up to the lighthouse as the afternoon waned. He detoured to the side to check the spot where the monster had left claw marks, and found the new, charred marks there too. He also found a little tuft of red, stuck to a bush. When he plucked it up he saw it was a feather, but the short, fluffy sort found on a bird's body, not a wing feather. He stroked the tuft of soft fluff—small compared to the ones he'd found before, but still huge for what it was. It was brilliant red all over, an almost unnatural shade. He tucked it into one of his many pockets with a shrug and continued on his way.

The door to the cottage opened almost as soon as Nico knocked, and Azrael practically tackled him with a hug.

Nico was surprised, but not unhappy. He willingly hugged back. "Miss me?"

"More than I expected. I worried, too. This monster out there . . . What if you ran into it?"

"Well, that's my job." Nico smiled and extracted himself from Azrael's embrace.

"Yes, but . . ." Azrael stopped and shook his head. "I just worried, that's all. It's almost time for me to light the lamp, though. Do you want to come with me?"

"No way." Nico grinned. "I thought I'd just watch the sunset, actually. It's a really nice day, so why not? Then I can help you with breakfast, or dinner, or whatever meal it is."

"Sure, that sounds lovely." Azrael smiled, and went up on his toes to give Nico a quick kiss, then turned away, blushing, and went inside.

Nico chuckled. It seemed that now Azrael had been introduced to kissing, he was very bold about it. He turned from the lighthouse, looking out over the ocean and surveying the head for a good spot to sit. He settled on a rock near the garden, where he could see the long, rolling waves come wash against the shore, red sunset light rippling over them. They foamed high up on the beach, for it was high tide, and he could hear the boom as they crashed against the head itself, nearly beneath his feet.

The lighthouse's beam suddenly came on, adding a cooler, golden-white light to the shimmer across the waves, which seemed to get brighter as the sun slowly vanished into the sea. Soon there was only a hint of warm purple in the sky, and a touch of pink on a few lingering puffs of cloud, while the stars were appearing above and the lighthouse became the brightest thing in the sky.

Nico rose slowly, dusting himself off, and turned to head inside.

It was a good thing he'd done so, or he would have been tackled off the edge of the cliff when something dove down out of the sky at him. Instead, turning let him glimpse it in time to throw himself flat, and it went by overhead, moving too fast to change its course.

As Nico rose into a crouch and looked after it he could see, by the lighthouse's light, that it was almost certainly the thing he'd been hunting. Bright, intense cherry red all over, with a pair of huge wings, it was the size of a car, easily. It had legs—arms?—like a bird's as well, scaled and taloned, also red, and the claws literally glowed against the dark night sky. Its head was birdlike but with a higher forehead, which made room for three eyes, all three of them bright gold. Instead of hind legs or a tail, though, it had a cluster of tentacles, like the lower half of an octopus, though he thought there might be more than eight. Nico wasn't about to bother counting them, though, he was too busy sprinting towards the cottage.

The massive thing pivoted in the air with surprising dexterity and dove down again. Nico flung himself flat and sideways, but it wasn't enough; he felt burning talons clip his shoulder as he went down. The monster apparently got too low in the process, though, for it crashed to the ground ahead of him, going head-over-tentacles in a tumble through the garden.

It lunged upright with a screech while Nico, trying to ignore the pain searing through his shoulder, got to his knees, scrabbling to get inside his coat to a particular pocket.

There was a scream like a hawk's, high overhead, and something dark plunged from the top of the lighthouse to land on the monster's back, driving it to the ground.

Nico froze, watching, as the new arrival—precisely like the first in shape and size, but jet black and with purple eyes—bit and clawed at the other creature. The latter reached up with burning claws, lashing at its attacker. The attacker lashed back, its claws as black as the rest of it, lacking the hot-iron fire of the first. It was also attacking with only one hand, for the other was curled in on itself, its claws useless, the scaled arm above it seamed with silvery scars.

Nico felt as though his heart stopped beating for an instant as everything snapped into place.

In the same moment Nico's scrabbling hand reached the right pocket and he pulled out his Colt 1911 and centered it on the red creature. It was thrashing and rolling, tangled so closely with the dark monster—with Azrael—that it was impossible to get a clear shot.

"Hey!" Nico shouted, and for just an instant both creatures turned to look at him.

He fired the gun, squeezing the trigger twice, aiming right at the center of the triangle made by the red monster's triple eyes.

It whipped its head back, shrieking and thrashing, but it was no longer a coordinated attempt to fight, it was merely pained flailing, and

Azrael took instant advantage of that, the claws of his left hand ripping across the red monster's throat.

The creature made a hideous bubbling sound, half collapsing. Azrael hissed like a teakettle, a whistling shriek of rage, and clawed at it again and again, until it was still and unmoving, dark liquid that must be blood pooling beneath it.

With a snarl and a heave, Azrael pushed it over, its tentacles giving a few twitches, showing it wasn't completely dead yet, and shoved it off the cliff, into the churning ocean below.

Then Azrael collapsed with a whine of pain, lying flat, his wings splayed out, his own tentacles shuddering and curling.

Nico pulled himself slowly to his feet and stuffed the gun back in his pocket. He staggered over to Azrael, his shoulder still utter agony, and reached out hesitantly to the groaning monster.

"Hey . . . You, uh, are you okay?"

Azrael twisted his head around, three huge purple eyes looking at Nico. A weird burbling, trilling sound came from him. It was hard to tell how wounded he was, for the wounds were charred black, nearly invisible against his black feathers. Suddenly, though, a shudder went through him, his body seeming to ripple like a heat wave. It pulled in, black fading to pale, and then the Azrael Nico knew, a short, handsome man dressed in frumpy, too-big clothing, lay groaning on the grass. Nico knelt beside him. He still couldn't see much; the injuries seemed to be beneath Azrael's clothing.

Nico helped Azrael sit up, worry running through him. How badly injured was his . . . his what? Lover? Quarry? Whatever he was, though, Nico couldn't leave him like this.

"You good to walk?" asked Nico.

"I think so." Azrael got his feet under him, and Nico helped him get upright, supporting him as he limped to the lighthouse cottage.

Inside, Nico pulled Azrael's sweater and shirt off, wincing as he saw the multiple charred gouges beneath. They were smaller than the marks across his own shoulder, some odd effect of Azrael's shape-changing, but they persisted, and Nico insisted on Azrael sitting down and letting him clean them out. The heat had cauterized them, so at least infection was probably not a problem, but the burns themselves were bad, making Nico frown. None of them were horribly deep, but they were worrying, especially after Azrael admitted there were more and pulled his pants off, revealing a number of charred slashes across his legs.

"I'll be alright," said Azrael. "Really. Just wash them out, it'll be fine. I should look at yours too, they're pretty deep."

"Okay."

Nico hissed in pain when Azrael washed out the three slashes across his shoulder. They weren't bleeding, but they hurt like hell. Azrael insisted on bandaging them up, though he'd refused such for his own injuries. With soft cloth wound around his shoulder, Nico was at least able to focus on something other than the pain, though that lingered in the background all the same.

"So, ah, it turns out you're the monster," he said, finally. "Or one of the monsters."

Azrael sighed and looked down into his lap. "Yes."

"I . . ." Nico trailed off, not knowing what to say.

"Do you hate me?" said Azrael, his voice small, his body hunched and curled in.

"No! Of course not!"

Azrael let out a soft sigh. "That's good. I *am* sorry, but I hope you understand why I couldn't tell you."

"I do, yes. Can you explain what's been going on, though? You left the first set of marks. This other, red creature like you left the second . . . and you don't like each other at all. That's all I know."

"Hah. Yes, I suppose you wouldn't make the other connections. I said, once, that I'd been betrothed. It's . . . it's not quite the same as marriage, we don't do things that way, but it's a loose analogue. Our families were to be bound, with that other and I as symbols of it. The other, she . . . We're not gendered as humans are? I've been calling her my fiancée, though, so . . . She wanted it, and I didn't. So I tried to flee. She caught me on the borders, the boundaries, and did this." He lifted his scarred hand. "But I escaped, and tried to make a life here."

"I see. That sounds rough."

"The first few years were comically absurd. I had no idea how humans did anything, and I confused and unnerved any number of people. Then I found books; and stumbled on the lighthouse job. Sixteen years of reading and making small, careful attempts to speak with the few people who came up here, and I felt I had at least some small grasp on how to act like a human. Enough so that when a stranger showed up at my door I didn't send him away." He smiled at Nico.

"I'm glad of that," said Nico.

"Are you? Still? Knowing what I am?"

"Of course! You're still the same person. Having another shape doesn't change that!"

Azrael's smile was like sunlight, the brightest smile Nico had ever seen on him. "Oh! I'm so glad! Thank you."

"But . . . So you ended up here, living quietly. Why the sudden appearance? Why draw all that attention?"

"I saw . . . Not saw? Sensed? Felt? Whatever it was, I saw *her* while I was out flying one night. I try to live as a human, but flying is so . . ." Azrael shrugged. "It's hard to give up. So I was out flying along the shoreline when I caught a glimpse of her. Just for a moment, but I could see she'd found this world, and was testing the boundaries. I hoped that marking this place as mine, all along the edges where the world-barriers are thinner, would show her that she should keep away. Obviously that didn't work, though. Her putting her own marks over mine, higher up, was a challenge. Perhaps I should have answered it immediately, but . . . I was still hoping to somehow settle this without conflict. She's so much bigger than me . . ."

Nico frowned. "Higher? Bigger? Her claw marks were directly over yours, and you seemed to be the same size."

"Oh, no, uhm . . . It's hard to put into English. Not higher in a physical sense. Higher . . . energy, I suppose? That's why she's red. Red is more energetic than black? The way stars are? I'm sorry, I could explain this better if I weren't so tired, I'm sure. She's . . . higher, so she has more heat than I do. I'm not big enough or old enough to have any heat, I just have myself, so I'm black. My parents were yellow and blue! Very strong people! But I'm only black, I'm nothing much."

Nico frowned, trying to parse through that. It made a strange sort of sense. "So you mean . . . bigger is like hotter, in your world?"

"Yes! Not just hotter, *more* in many ways. But yes. She only wanted me because of my family, I'm nothing special. I hoped that meant she'd leave me alone. I guess not. I . . . She's certainly dead now, though. We're tough creatures, but what you did, and what I did, and the ocean . . . Water doesn't mix well with her sort of energy. So she's gone, and I'm free, if my parents are willing to leave me alone."

He smiled at Nico then. "So thank you. I'd never have beaten her without your help. She was so much bigger, and I only have full use of the one hand. But you gave me the opening I needed, and now I'm free."

"I'm glad," said Nico simply.

"You're not . . . angry, or sickened that we . . . that I took advantage of you thinking I was human? That you made love to a monster?"

"Tch." Nico scoffed, shaking his head. "Of course not! That's something you learn, monster hunting, is that people are people. Obviously they can't be allowed to run around committing murder, but come on. I don't care what you look like, you're yourself, in any form."

"Oh, Nico . . ." Azrael wrapped his arms around Nico, gentle but firm, and kissed him.

Nico kissed back, warm and fervent. This was all strange, certainly, but he'd meant it when he'd said that people were people. Azrael was still the person he'd come to know, even if he also sometimes had wings and tentacles.

When they broke apart, though, Azrael flopped back on the bed. "I am all done in."

Nico sprawled beside him. "Yeah. Time to sleep?"

Azrael sighed. "The light?"

"It's on now. Would it be the end of the world if you were late putting it out?"

"I . . . Something could go wrong . . ."

"How often does that happen?" Nico gave Azrael an amused look. He was so serious, so dutiful, even after all this.

"Oh, well . . . Hardly ever. Maybe half a dozen times since I've been here?"

"Less than once a year. Feh. Sleep. We'll sort out whatever else needs sorting come morning."

Azrael hesitated, then he sighed. "You're right."

They got themselves tucked together into the bed. It wasn't all that large, so they had to cuddle close, but neither of them objected. Azrael tucked his head beneath Nico's chin, and Nico put an arm over Azrael, and as they rested together in the darkness, broken only by the glimmer of the lighthouse beam outside the window, it was easy for them to find rest in each other's arms.

<hr />

Nico woke alone in the bed, but he could hear Azrael bustling at the kitchen end of the room, and when he sat up, Azrael said, "Good morning. Tea?"

"Yeah, that sounds great." Nico stretched, then winced. God, he was going to have some epic scars later, but right now his shoulder hurt like hell. Getting a cup of tea inside him didn't do anything for the pain, but Azrael dug out some aspirin, and that helped. Nico noticed that Azrael was no longer limping.

"Looks like you're feeling better?" he ventured.

Azrael gave a sheepish little shrug. "After I put the light out, I spent some time in the lighthouse in my other form. I heal faster that way. So yes. I wish I could do the same for you."

Nico shrugged, then winced. Right, no shrugging. "I'll live."

"Is there anything else I can do for you?" asked Azrael, brows drawn together in concern.

"Eh. Not really." He smiled, then added, "Give me a kiss?"

Azrael laughed. "As many as you like." He came over and gently put his hands on Nico's waist, going up on his toes to give Nico a kiss.

"Mmm." Nico bent and kissed back. When they broke apart, though, he couldn't help but indulge his curiosity. "You said you were small in your people's terms. Is that why you're short as a human?"

"I think so, yes."

"So your ex-fiancée would be very tall?"

"Oh no, she'd be merely average. My parents would be tall, though, my . . . mother, I suppose, especially so."

"Huh. Forgive me if I ask too many questions. I don't often get the chance to learn these sorts of things. Usually the, ah . . . 'monsters' aren't very fond of me."

Azrael chuckled. "I'm *quite* fond of you. Ask all the questions you like, I don't mind."

"Would it be alright to ask to see your other form?"

"Of course. Not in here, though. It doesn't fit very well in here." He opened the door to the lighthouse, Nico trailing behind him. "Stand over by the door, please," said Azrael, and Nico, after closing the door, did so.

Azrael suddenly wavered like a heat shimmer, blurring, swelling, and darkening, and then there was a massive creature standing in the center of the lighthouse, taking up most of the clear space there.

He stood on perhaps a dozen black-skinned tentacles, smooth rather than suckered, and tapering to tiny tips, though his weight rested short of those. They curved back up again from where they touched the ground, and waved and twisted gently around each other in an absent fidgeting sort of motion. A deep-keeled torso was above those, covered all over in sleek, jet-black feathers, and two long arms supported it. Azrael's overall posture reminded Nico of a gorilla, bent forward to rest on his clawed hands, though only on one of them; he carried the other tucked up, the scars far more visible against the black scales than they'd been on his fair human skin.

Two huge wings were folded along his sides, the tips of the primaries standing out well behind him, and his head was very much like a raven's, with a long, straight beak, but the shape of his skull was more rounded, and of course he had three eyes, two set on the sides and one above and in the center, all of them a vivid amethyst purple. His head was easily ten feet up, and his whole body bulked many, many times Nico's size. He shouldn't, in fact, have been able to fly, despite the size of his wings, but of course he was obviously not quite bound by this world's laws.

He tilted his head to the side, making a deep but recognizably birdlike questioning sound, and Nico almost laughed. He'd thought, when he first met Azrael, that the way he did that made him seem like a bird. Now it was obvious where the habit came from.

"You can't speak like this?" said Nico.

Azrael shook his head, then made a series of rumbling noises alternating with higher sounds that were nearly chirps. The patterns were definitely complicated enough to convey some kind of meaning.

"Ah. You can, but not English, hmm?"

Azrael nodded.

"Is it alright if I touch you?"

Azrael nodded again, so Nico stepped forward. He couldn't resist touching Nico's scarred arm first, feeling the smooth scales and the different texture of the silver scars that interrupted them. Scars had always interested him, the marks of people's past. He had more than a few of his own, after all. On impulse Nico kissed one, at the "elbow" of Azrael's arm since he couldn't reach any higher than that.

To his surprise, Azrael made a soft trilling sound that was almost a purr. When Nico looked up he saw that all three of Azrael's eyes were lidded, his expression, as much as he had one, relaxed. Nico stroked over the scars again, and left another kiss before exploring along Azrael's feathered side. He caressed over the part of the wing that he could reach, the feathers there not as soft, but smooth and sleek.

"Huh. Do you have to groom your feathers?"

Azrael nodded again, with a little clack of his beak, which revealed the fact that he had an almost canine array of sharp white teeth inside it, very much unlike any earthly bird.

"I imagine that's a lot of work."

A deep, rumbling chuckle answered that, along with another nod.

Nico touched one of the tentacles. It was warm under his hand, though he'd half expected it to be cold. The skin was smooth and a little rubbery. It reminded him of holding a snake, but smoother and warmer. It was almost soft, and entirely pleasant. One of the tentacles nearest him lifted and curled its tip around his hand. The end of it was as narrow as Nico's own smallest finger, though at the top each tentacle was as big around as his own leg. He held still as it crawled up his arm, squeezing. It was obviously very strong, but its touch was carefully delicate.

"Huh. That feels weird."

Azrael chuckled again, and Nico felt another touch, this time at his waist. He was wearing only his undershorts and the bandage around his chest and shoulder, so the tentacle touched bare skin there. It curled around him tightly.

"What are you up to?" Nico gave Azrael an amused look. Azrael trilled, his expression looking pleased, and another tentacle curled around Nico's waist, just above the first. Then all at once he was lifted up in the air, startling him into letting out a yelp.

Azrael trilled laughter and brought Nico up to his face. His beak was big enough to bite Nico in half, but he merely nuzzled the tip of it against Nico's cheek, still trilling in pleasure and amusement.

Nico laughed and turned his head to put a kiss on the side of Azrael's beak. "Having fun?"

Another trill and a little bobbing nod answered him.

"Could you put me down now, please?"

Azrael gently lowered Nico to the ground, but didn't let go of him. Instead he lowered himself too, lying on his back, wings still tucked to his sides. He pulled Nico in to lie on his feathered chest, and gently placed his left hand on Nico's back. He was so delicate about it that he didn't even jar Nico's injured shoulder, despite the fact that the taloned fingers of Azrael's hand were longer than Nico's whole forearm.

"Wanting to cuddle, hmm?"

"Chrrrp!"

"I'll take that as a yes."

With another little trill Azrael started curling more tentacles around Nico, until he was nearly covered in them. It might have felt frightening, he was in a certain sense completely restrained and helpless, but instead it felt protective and comforting. He trusted Azrael. They'd saved each other's lives only last night. There was no need to fear, wrapped in such a warm embrace.

Although the ends of Azrael's tentacles were still fidgeting around, possibly some unconscious movement, and given how thoroughly Nico was wrapped up in them, he found himself having a reaction to one coiled around his upper thigh in particular. He ground his hips down against Azrael for a moment, and all the tentacles went still. "If you keep that up, you're going to start something," noted Nico with a chuckle of his own. "Which isn't a complaint, I'm just warning you. That feels a little too good."

Azrael's answering trill was almost a giggle. He nuzzled against Nico's cheek with the very tip of his beak, and then the tentacle around his thigh very slowly, deliberately squirmed there, rubbing at the thin fabric of his undershorts.

Nico groaned and ground his hips down again. His cock was already starting to harden just from that. The situation he was in was weird, but he liked Azrael, and there was no denying the teasing touch felt good.

All the tentacles tightened around Nico for a moment, making his breath hitch. Then Azrael gently picked him up and turned him over onto his back, laying him back down with his head on Azrael's chest, and his legs resting over the upper parts of his tentacles. The ends of them curled and shifted, holding him in a snug embrace again, but now in addition to the ones wrapped around his legs, one bold tentacle tip wiggled its way under the waistband of Nico's undershorts. Nico gasped, then moaned as it curled around the base of his cock. "Oh . . . fuck . . . That is really weird."

Azrael halted, and Nico managed to say, "No, I mean it's good. It's just different, but please, don't stop."

Azrael trilled, nearly in Nico's ear, nuzzling and nibbling gently at his hair now. The tentacle caressing Nico's cock wound its way up the whole of it, coiling around it from root to tip, and squeezed lightly, which made Nico moan. That seemed to encourage Azrael, for he started stroking, working firmly up and down along Nico's cock. Nico closed his eyes, head tipped back, and gave himself over to it. He couldn't move anyway, all he could do was lie there and let his strange lover pleasure him.

The tentacle kept a steady pace, stroking slowly, sending pleasure washing through Nico. As it went on, though, it started to feel like a tease. "Ah . . . Azrael . . . Please, faster . . ."

With another trill Azrael responded, increasing his pace. Nico moaned and tried to buck into the strokes, his pleasure building. "Yeah . . . Oh, fuck, yeah . . ."

Azrael let out a little whine, followed by a huff, beak tugging at Nico's hair more sharply. He was breathing faster himself, Nico realized, the feathered chest beneath him rising and falling rapidly. The tentacle stroked faster still, and all other thoughts left Nico's head as he shuddered on the edge. "Yes . . . Azrael . . . Ah, yes!" With a cry and a profound shudder he came, hot seed spurting out into Azrael's grip.

As Nico slowly relaxed, Azrael heaved a sigh beneath him. The tentacle curled around Nico's cock slowly withdrew, somehow not leaving any mess behind, so it must have . . . eaten it somehow? Nico's mind was too hazed with pleasure for him to puzzle over that much. Azrael kept him embraced otherwise, tentacles curled around him, a huge, clawed hand gently stroking over Nico's chest, while he gave another affectionate nuzzle to Nico's cheek. His trill was questioning, and Nico answered with, "That was very good. Weird. But good. Mmm."

Azrael gave another trill that sounded smugly satisfied. Then he started unwinding his grip, and guided Nico to slide off of him and find his footing—wobbly at first—on the floor. A moment later Azrael had shimmered and shrunk down to human shape, dressed as he'd been in his usual sweater and slacks. "I take it I did alright?" he said.

"Definitely," was Nico's immediate response. He came over and folded his arms around Azrael, moving the one shoulder carefully, but not much minding the twinge of pain, he was still feeling too good.

He nuzzled into Azrael's hair and added, "Now next time I just have to figure out what to do for you."

"Oh, er . . ." Nico could nearly hear Azrael's blush. "I mean, that will probably be even weirder . . . Uhm . . ."

"I don't mind the weird. Assuming you still want me coming around?" he added, feeling a sudden flare of worry. Perhaps now that he wasn't worried about his ex, Azrael wouldn't want Nico about anymore.

"You are always welcome here," said Azrael instantly, hugging Nico tightly. "Always."

All Nico could do was hug Azrael back.

About the Author

S. *Park* began writing at age six, and it's been an enjoyable activity ever since. Several of his stories have been published by the furry and fantasy small press Jaffa Books. He currently has several novels and numerous short stories out in several different genres. He tries to write interesting stories using his own life experiences, as filtered through the "anything is possible" lens of science fiction and fantasy.

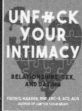